The Blood Red Box

Brian Kelly Irons

First Edition Published 2021 by Bob Scott Publishing

www.facebook.com/BobScottPublishing

ISBN: 9781952819124

To my love, Debra… Your support and inspiration have never faltered.

Prelude

1955

Bethany sat lazily on a mound of dirt in her bare feet playing with the drop of blood emerging on her index finger. The blood was brought about from a sewing needle that she employed to puncture her own skin. She poked and poked until a bubble of red emerged. She enjoyed the pain and squeezed the tip for a larger yield. The blood stained her dress as it dripped off her finger. The early afternoon air was hot and wet with humidity. She had been out there since the early morning hours, wanting to be alone with the birds as they kidnapped the worms from the dewy soil. A rumble of commotion could be heard from inside the house and she smiled slightly. From behind her, she heard the slap of the screen door as it closed and she smiled wider as she listened to the rustle of grass and the approach of her sister, Beatrice.

"Beth!" yelled Beatrice, coming around to face her. "Mom told me what you did, you bitch."

"And what did I do, Bea?"

“You know exactly what you did. You tore up my new shoes and cut holes in my skirt. They are completely unwearable now and you did it on purpose.”

Beatrice was in a rage. She held the damaged items in her arms. Her face was red with anger and she tossed the skirt and the shoes at her sister’s feet. Bethany was startled momentarily but then laughed at her sister’s misfortune. She was always happy laughing at misfortune, especially her sister’s.

Beatrice and Bethany Kleinfeldt were twins; identical twins. From the moment they were born they seemed to have a knack for competition. It was usually harmless: who would get dressed quicker, which one finished their dinner first; until recently. Bethany began to display a behavior that one might consider to be violent. One moment she would be calm and still and then the next moment she was tearing the wallpaper from the walls – laughing as she did so.

When Beatrice began to excel in her studies, Bethany took this as a direct threat. Instead of having her own success in school, Bethany chose the opposite. She would often go for days without going to school – hiding in a park nearby and often not returning home for weeks at a time.

"And why should I care at all about your precious skirt and shoes? Nobody cares. I did us all a favor. Mom and Dad were sick to death, having to hear about your stupid play. None of us are going anyway so why does it even matter? All you care about are your stupid clothes and your stupid school. You think you're so much smarter than me, don't you? Sweet little Beatrice and all your good grades and perfect friends. You think that you're so much better than everyone else. You make me sick to my stomach."

There was a brief moment of silence, no more than a second or two as Beatrice attempted to regain her composure. Her relationship with her sister had never been warm and loving but, once the girls turned twelve, their personalities drove them both in completely different directions. Beatrice entered middle school with high expectations and a goal of perfect attendance. Bethany, on the other hand, cared nothing for school and was often truant. She shirked her chores at home and grew disrespectful to her parents. Their mother received most of the harshness and hurtful attitudes. While her father was left to much of the discipline, he often allowed her temperament to pass, claiming passively that she was going through a phase that she would one day grow out of.

"Just stay away from me, Beth. Understand me? Stay away."

Beatrice stormed off back to the house leaving Bethany to her bloody finger. She smiled again at her work. She felt no love for her sister or her family or remorse for what she had done. She was happy to have caused her sister so much dismay. *Bea hadn't cried, though.* This thought upset her somewhat. She wished that she had said something to make her cry. She stood, dusted the dirt off of her dress and walked away – into the woods behind their house, barefoot and sucking the blood from her finger.

Today

Good day to you. Or good evening; whichever the situation may be for you at the moment. My name is Walter Kirk, and boy, do I ever have a story to tell you. I wish this were one of those run-of-the-mill memoirs with their daily affirmations and the check-the-box type of narrative. Or perhaps a super-market tabloid romance, with the constant push and pull of so much dramatic emotional distress. Even better, the popular dragon slayer fantasy that never ends quite the way you wish it to. Alas, it is not.

It is certainly not my intention to scare you either or push you into the arms of a different author, but I feel the need to warn you: this tale I have weaved is not for the faint of heart. As much as I would wish it to be a happy story, or even a normal one, I refuse the pretension of narcissistic embellishment. It is, however, an autobiography of a short moment in time; a small portion of my life. A life that, prior to the events described within these pages, was wonderfully normal. At first, I was repulsed with the idea of putting this whole account to paper. Who would believe such a thing? What person in their right mind could ever accept that the events herein are anything but factual? The longer I mulled it over, the more I came to realize that writing this allegory would be more for me than anything else. A sort of cathartic show-and-tell into my land of reality vs. make believe. A prize fight that you must decide the outcome.

I made the conscious decision to write this story after an evening of bourbon and cheese with a group of school friends. I had been asked to relate the story after a conversation regarding the whereabouts of my sister Jillian were inquired. Arnold Putnam, after all these years, expressed to me that he had had a crush on her – his first crush as a matter of fact. I will attempt here to tell you the story that I told them, with some added detail as it comes to me. You must forgive the disconnection of events, however. My mind recalls only in the order that I remember them.

So, grab your coffee, turn the lights back on and have the children leave the room. I'll wait.

Ready? Very well then; I shall continue.

Now, I consider myself a reasonable guy with a reasonable existence. I had a great job with a great firm. Intellectual Property law was not glamorous but it's the most lucrative of legal careers. I had a wonderful flat on the west side of Herald Circle – looking out over the park. I cooked all my own meals and enjoyed doing so. I rode my bicycle at least two hours every day. I took walks around the neighborhood and spent my money locally. I listened to music with passion and drove my car with respect. In simple terms: I loved my life. I had everything a single man could ever want.

Precisely one week after my fortieth birthday, amidst the fog of a four-day long party that left me with a headache so severe that I swear to you was a living thing, something happened to me. What that something is I will get to later but suffice it to say: I changed. And by changed I don't mean that I altered my hairstyle. That would be impossible, given that I've been nearly bald for many years. Nor did I enter into a fitness membership. Could you imagine me in spandex standing narcissistically in front of a full-length mirror, flexing? No, what changed was the perception of my own reality. I no longer knew the difference between what was real and what was being played out in my mind like a film.

As I write this, I must take into consideration what you might possibly be thinking, but you must believe me when I tell you that even the most unbelievable points of what you are about to read actually happened.

Let's start with Penelope, and the moment I realized that something was a bit, how shall I put it? Off?

I did nothing

Penelope was choking. Her eyes searched for me. I had assumed that there was something stuck in her throat, something that blocked the flow of air. She appeared to be in distress, and yet for some strange reason, I did nothing to assist. I wanted to, you see. I wanted to put down the knife and fork and relinquish the glass of Alexander Valley Cabernet Sauvignon. At $185 a glass, I should've put it down carefully. Yet I sat still in my seat, the muscles in my hands were no longer under my control. I sat frozen in horror as my beloved Penelope turned blue. She gasped for air but none came. She clasped her slender hands around her neck in the universal choking gesture. And still, I did nothing. If I remember correctly, I actually picked up my napkin and wiped my mouth.

From out of the corner of my unwavering eye came a man. Adorned in all black so I assumed he was a member of the wait staff. Penelope's eyes strained to gain my attention as the server with a neatly trimmed goatee picked her up and held her about the waist. He wrapped his arms around her and thrusted her abdomen until a piece of unchewed fillet came flying out of her mouth and landed with a splash on the floor. She inhaled with desperation. The entire dining room turned to me with astonished anger. Penelope leaned on the back of the leather chair to gain her balance then sat down on it to reintroduce her lungs to oxygen. She glared at me and I bristled; marginally unaware of the situation around me.

"What's the matter with you?" she yelled. At first, I didn't fully comprehend the question. She had never once raised her voice at me so I'm sure you can imagine how shocked I was. A fork full of smoked salmon in my right hand and a glass of Cabernet in my left, I quickly came spinning back to reality and I scanned the scene before me. I opened my mouth to attempt an explanation but was instantly halted by an unwarranted bout of dumbfoundedness. The customers looked like they were ready to lay siege upon me. Expletives were slung like hash on a paper plate.

"Are you alright, my darling?" I reached for her hand and she recoiled.

"Don't you ever touch me again!"

She stood. The chair behind her toppled to the floor with a crash.

She looked down at it, embarrassed. I had never seen her this angry before. I was frightened. Even more so when she pulled at the long rope of pearls around her neck – balls of white shimmering luminescence bouncing from the table to the floor. The pearls…

I plucked one from the linen and held it up to allow the light to shine from it. It was perfect. I knew nothing of pearls, but my plan to have them appraised was still in effect. I pocketed the single sphere and stood dizzily from the table. The soft silk braid that held them was now stained purple from the wine the event had spilled. Penelope ran, crying. I did not give chase. I returned to my plate and finished my meal. There was still a single swallow of wine remaining, but the capers seemed a bit over cooked.

The pearls. I felt a pang to my heart. We had found them nearly two hours ago. She smiled as wide as the sun that her eyes reflected. We had taken the entire day to spend together. My work schedule didn't always allow for free time, so we took advantage of it when it was offered. She said she wanted to go shopping; antique shopping, of course, I promised. And why not? I held a particular affinity for antiques and if it made my Penelope happy, well then that's what we would do.

The city was bursting with the smells and colors of springtime. It was even warmer than we had expected, so we chose to walk about the cobbled shopping district in lieu of my car, which I so loved to drive. But seeing her happy meant more to me than horsepower and black leather. The square was alive with people – a grand time to be in love in the city. A small farmers market caressed our palettes with fresh sprigs of thyme and dill. Penelope purchased a few bunches of parsley and cilantro and we moved on.

At the corner of Menlo Avenue and 52nd, we turned and strolled along the antique purveyors. Wise shop owners placed their more popular items outside for the lure of what might be found within. It was as if some absurd shopping mall had at once dropped its walls. It wasn't actually as bad as all that, especially with the sight of a group of food trucks offering a plethora of deliciousness. This is where we set our course.

We stepped inside a tiny shop called Wentworth & Smithburg – specializing in unique, hard to find historical items. Outside of number of rare books and lithographs, crystal was the clear item of choice for the owners of this shop and we tiptoed in and out – uninterested. Next was a rare bookseller. Anyone who claims to know me knows that it's near impossible to pull me from a bookstore, yet, with a smile, Penelope shook her head and led me further down the lane. I made a mental note to slip inside before we left. The next shop was a candle maker, and then more fancy crystal. These were easy to pass. Not that I was uninterested in candles you see, but certain smells took me back to a place that I was not prepared to visit.

At the end of the lane stood an unadorned shop with no visible name. Looking through the dusty window, we spied very little of interest, but we shrugged and ventured inside. A muted bell rang upon our reluctant entry and Penelope took quick notice that the heavily padded carpeting had to be over a hundred years old. The bright sunlight that was ever present outside did not have the strength to penetrate the dust and years of grime on the windows. The smell of age and mold hung on everything. Dust was everywhere and I thought of my sister Jillian and her allergies. The items on display were old, yes, but there was nothing that drew our attention. Shelves of oddities covered each wall. Objects that, though clearly antique, could not possibly return a profit. I kissed my darling Penelope softly on the cheek and took her hand. She smiled and nodded. We turned to exit the establishment.

"Pardon me, sir," a voice boomed from beyond a cluttered counter.

"Yes?" I answered, and a small man wearing a black suit with a purple turban and matching bow tie walked towards us. The suit was expensive; Italian most likely. The turban was encrusted with jewels throughout. He displayed a chain attached from a nose ring to a group of golden hoops on both ears.

"I believe you came here for this." His voice contained an accent that was unfamiliar to me. If I had to guess I would say that it was a Middle Eastern dialect. In his hands, he carried a wooden box. At the moment I paid no attention to this. I was more intrigued by his diminutive stature. From sight, he was between four and four and a half feet tall. A beard of total gray hung to his waist with a single braid, held together at the end by a golden bell.

"I don't understand," I told him. "We're not interested, sir. You have a lovely shop, but we really must be going. Thank you."

The man brushed passed us with a speed that even now I'm incapable of understanding. He stood before the door as if blocking our egress. The box that he held in his small hands was nearly as wide as he was.

"This is for you, sir." He raised the item above his head, and I was forced to take notice. The box was red with a glossy finish that shone brighter than anything else in the shop. It was roughly twelve inches wide, and half as much tall. The trim and hinges were polished brass. But what I took notice of more than any other was the clasp. It wasn't brass but more of a dull silver or perhaps a brushed nickel or platinum. It was fashioned in the shape of a wild boar's head, and I can tell you without the slightest hesitation that upon viewing the clasp, I knew that the box truly was for me, if not already mine. I'm not certain how or why I know that, but I just do.

I smiled. "What's the price?" Penelope turned her face to me and laughed. I'm sure that she thought that I was buying the thing simply to remove the man-child from in front of us. But there was something ancient about the item that held me captivated. Again, I cannot express to you the feeling I had at that moment. Had I seen this item before?

"Oh, you misunderstand, sir. The box is yours. I am only here to give it to you."

He bowed his head and held the box higher. I saw my reflection in its surface and placed my hands gracefully on its sides and lifted it from the dwarf's hands. Something within the box shifted; as if there were a living thing inside. If I hadn't felt it myself, I wouldn't have believed it. Once I touched the box, there were no more questions regarding its ownership. My fingers coursed with electromagnetic energy and I felt my skin become warm. A sound not unlike a whisper expelled from inside the shop and I looked at Penelope and then down to our new short friend, but it didn't appear that they had heard it. I know it sounds crazy, but I believed that the object was speaking to me. The small man was correct. It belonged to me. The same as my car or my house, and I walked out happily, with my darling Penelope on my arm.

Christmas Eve

1955

The floorboards creaked and the jingle bells attached to the banister danced in the breeze from the furnace and Bethany tiptoed down the hall to her parents' room. She looked back in utter disgust at the presents placed joyfully under the Christmas tree. The last Christmas that she enjoyed was three years ago. She had wanted a doll so dearly; one that she could talk to, one with real eyes that opened and closed. Instead, she got the ugliest yellow dress that the world had ever seen. Beatrice got the doll, of course. Beatrice always got what she wanted, and Bethany got the leftovers. She had thought first about putting her slippers on but knew that the slap on the wood floor would wake up her brother Mark. A distraction such as that would not do. Instead, she slipped on a pair of fluffy socks to soften her steps.

As she got closer, she felt a bit of apprehension rise in her chest; could she really go through with it? She hesitated. She would go to jail. That was a chance she would have to take. She persevered. This needed to happen. She didn't care what they did to her. It was important that she stuck to her guns and followed through. She stepped passed Beatrice's room and spat on her door – smiling at the thought of sweet perfect Beatrice waking up to see a gob of saliva on her door. She would spit at her face if she didn't think that it would wake her. She approached her parents' bedroom door; the slower the better. That was her plan. Sweat glistened on her arms and forehead as she cautiously twisted the knob. It creaked somewhat as metal engaged metal.

Bethany stood at the foot of her parents' bed and grimaced at the sight of them sleeping peacefully together. She remembered the first time that her father had touched her. She was only eight. He believed that she was sleeping. She didn't like the way that it felt, but he was her father. What could she do? She also remembered the first time she told her mother. She knew that her mother would protect her. That's what mothers are for. But she didn't. She didn't protect her child. Bethany's mother refused to believe that her husband was capable of such things and told her child that she would no longer hear anything about it. So, she pushed it down – deep – and left it there. At school, Bethany had the idea to tell her teacher, who in turn told her mother. Bethany was grounded and the incident forgotten, to all but Bethany.

Bethany felt her skin crawl and stepped lively to where her father slept and raised the steak knife that she gripped in her hand. She watched his chest rise as he breathed and told herself that he didn't deserve the oxygen. The grip on the knife tightened despite the increased feeling of uneasiness. Her father turned his head away from her and she had a perfect shot at his temple. This would end her years of suffering. With her elbows bent, she inhaled, and her mother sat straight up.

"Bethany, just what in the hell do you think you're doing?" her mother yelled – waking her father in the process. Bethany feigned sleepwalking, appearing frightened, and quickly dropped the knife. Assuming that they didn't see the weapon in the dark, she ran out crying back to her bedroom and locked the door.

The following morning, Bethany refused to talk about what had happened, saying only that she was in her bed asleep all night long. Like many other Christmas mornings, Bethany refused any and all presents, claiming that Christmas presents were bought simply to buy her love, and she would not return their affections. Her abhorrence for love caused a rift within her and the act or feeling of love became a completely foreign manifestation.

There were no more questions

Once at home I removed Penelope's clothes and pressed my body against hers. This was the moment that we had both been longing for. Our skin mingled and she moaned deeply as I entered her. I had wanted her all afternoon. Once that I had her, I was unwilling to relinquish. I wanted her to tell me to stop – to beg me; to insist that she had had enough. But that was not my Penelope. She was insatiable. She craved each thrust, each yank of her hair, and I was more than happy to accommodate.

The night had not yet matured into full dark, and the moon waxed silver and purple. Thinking on it now, I remember having the feeling that I had never before seen anything like it. What creates a purple moon? I've seen a harvest moon, with its oranges and browns signaling the coming of autumn. I've even seen a blood moon though I'm not quite sure what it means. But never in my life have I seen a purple moon until this very evening. The air around us smelled and felt of passion and I became aware of every breath, of every rise and fall of her chest. I knew her thoughts as if they were my own, as if I were saying them. I felt the intense heat from her body as if it were my own. I not only knew what she felt but felt what and how she was feeling. Her body writhed in ecstasy and I enjoyed her pleasure along with her as if her climax were my own. It was unnerving, to say the least; and over before we knew it. Laying in our bed, exhausted, I reached for the box resting on the night table next to me. It was a curious thing. It appeared ancient and yet so well cared for that it could have been manufactured that very day. If I hadn't known better, I would have sworn that the box was speaking to me; in a whisper from the grave, perhaps.

"Let's open it." Penelope's enthusiasm matched my own and we both smiled like children peeking at something unknown. I must admit, I was apprehensive at first, but what has ever gone wrong from opening a box? So, we sat up and opened it. I got the immediate impression that the clasp was refusing my attempts. There was a faint sound of a muffled explosion somewhere in the distance, something sonic perhaps, and I got the feeling that something bad had just happened to someone in the world and I stiffened unwillingly. The clearest way for me to explain is perhaps the myth of the ringing ears. Someone somewhere was thinking of me.

Fully opened, the box smelled of lilac. It was so strong that I inhaled as if I were holding a fresh bouquet. The smell of lilac always reminds me of my mother. I hold fond memories of when Mom would walk around the neighborhood, picking sprigs from bushes along the way. Once at home she would put one in a glass with water, then take the rest into the kitchen where she would press them. The aroma was intoxicating. To this day, whenever I smell lilac, I glance about to see where the bush is. Like Mom, I gather a few blossoms and take them home.

The inner walls and floor of the box were lovingly adorned with plush red velvet. It reminded me instantly of the velvet seat of an antique movie house. Directly under the lid, the wood was so highly glossed that my reflection seemed unreal, like there was too much detail, as though the reflection wasn't mine, but of someone entirely different.

"Will you take a look at these, Walter?" Penelope said as she lifted out a string of the most luxurious pearls that either of us had ever seen. Again, I am no expert on pearls or any other jewelry for that matter. But these, they were extraordinary.

“What a splendid occasion,” I told her. “We shall celebrate. Let’s go to Randolph’s. I have a need for smoked salmon and capers.”

“And wine,” she posted.

“Expensive wine, my dear Penelope.”

I would never see her again

I left Randolph's in haste, spurred with the notion that I would never see her again. Her lustrous blonde hair flecked with strands the color of a tropical beach. Her eyes, the palest blue, like an early morning summer. Her smile created a dimple on her left cheek. One dimple. Many times, when we were together during quiet hours, I would place my hand upon her cheek and feel the softness of it. I often wondered what that must have been like for her as a child. Children can be so horribly mean. Her ears were the very definition of perfection. She never had them pierced so you can understand me when I tell you they were flawless. She was flawless. My dear Penelope. I loved her. I'm sure I did. Had I told her as such? I do not remember. In fact, I had only told one other person that I loved them, but that remains another part of the story.

Off to my right, roughly a block away, close to Green Brook, I heard the distant ringing of a payphone. It was odd enough to make me remember that I had assumed that all the payphones downtown had been taken out. Since the advent of the cell phone, there had been a decline in payphone usage, and frankly, I thought they were quite an eyesore. So you can surely imagine how I might have taken notice of this one. To make the odd situation even stranger, north on Menlo stood yet another payphone booth, this with its phone ringing. I stood directly in front of Randolph's, glancing back and forth at both payphones – perplexed, when the cellphone in my jacket pocket began to ring. I pulled it out and spied the caller identification: restricted. Of course, I denied the caller and inserted my phone back into my jacket. It was then that I noticed the telephone at the valet station started to ring. Two floors above me, in an apartment I supposed, a phone rang. Then from the Russian deli across the street, and the shoe shop next to it. Before I had a moment to realize it, all the telephones around me were ringing off the hook – with no one answering them. With an uncomfortable sense of foreboding, I set my pace towards the payphone at Green Brook. Once I entered the box, it stopped, as did all the others, and I felt a sense of relief – sprinkled with a dash of silliness at my own overreactivity.

I reopened the folding door to leave when a single ring

announced itself. I turned back to hear another, then another. It was then that I would swear to you that every single blasted phone on the planet were ringing at the same time. If only to cease the cacophony, I picked up the earpiece reluctantly and answered.

"Hello?"

The voice on the other end of the line was muffled, and I was certain that I heard a woman crying. The voice, male to be sure, was spouting off directions. Not navigational directions but orders. Do this, then do that. But none of it made sense. The voice was barely audible. That is until right before I went to hang up.

"Do you understand me, Walter?" This time the caller was louder than before. Though he sounded like he was under water, I had no trouble deciphering the message.

"Who is this?" I asked. "And how do you know my name?"

There was no answer to this. The crying woman became louder and it was obvious to me that it was my Penelope. She sounded in extreme despair. I had been a fool. An uncaring fool and I needed to make it right.

"Penelope, my darling. I am so very sorry. I don't know what came over me."

"Walter," she said softly. "Don't trust h – "

"Penelope?" She had gone. But it seemed that the caller was not through with me.

"Walter." This was a third voice. Male, yet soft and non-threatening. Almost charming. "You are to do what you have been instructed. Do you understand? Your precious Penelope will live as long as you follow my directions." And with that, the call went silent; as did all the other phones as well. I wasn't given an opportunity to protest – to ask who had taken her and why. Was she alright? The nerve endings throughout my entire body began to tingle and I felt as if I may pass out. I steadied myself against the phone booth and took a number of much needed breaths, inviting more oxygen into my system.

The orders that I had been given made no immediate sense within any amount of rational calculations. It was as if I had been given instructions to build an object, yet the materials for the object were out of my reach. Another breath and I stood upright. Another and I was able to move again. Still weak but gaining strength.

My eyes focused on the nearly full, and still slightly purple moon above a clear cloudless sky and I headed in the direction that my mind instructed me to. My dear Penelope: I could still feel her as if she were here next to me. I saw her; like a dream within a pillow of a cloud, sitting on a white divan at the home of her parents. She was still crying. Sobbing actually. What had I done? Had I hurt her? I couldn't remember what had caused her to storm out of the restaurant but clearly it was my doing. I was oftentimes overreacting to things that were out of my control.

My stride lengthened as I walked with a clear purpose. What that purpose was I could not tell you, but something was drawing me away from the city and I became more and more unfamiliar with my surroundings. Mile upon ceaseless mile I walked. Mesmerized by the drone of my shoes on the pavement and the shrill of a distant motorway. A sudden chill took me over and I stopped to get my bearings. East, west; perhaps east. No, north. I had no idea really. One look at the moon and I knew even less. I shivered visibly at the cold and yet I felt the warmth of my darling Penelope. She was sitting near the fire in her father's den, working through a photo album – still crying. I felt the tears race down her cheeks. I instantly breathed in the scent of her hair. I reached out to caress her face and she quickly brought her hand to her cheek – brushing away my attempts at comforting her.

I walked. I walked a lonely maze of streets and alleys. Unsure why it was that I was there, in the night, when I was happy to be at home with my wine and the fire licking at my frozen toes. The walking seemed to warm them so I continued upon the path; a path that led to nowhere. The lavender moon following my every move. Rows upon rows of dirty lots and empty homes. Avenues of broken windows and unrequited dreams. Remnants of shattered lives scattered about the potholed streets. More than once I noticed a familiar street name or turn of the road. I had been here before, hadn't I? Pleasant Road, left, down two blocks to Palmer then right on Berkshire. Yes? Then five houses down on the left.

I felt a sickness upon me. The uneasiness of a hallucination that at first seemed so convincing but then turned on me like a wild animal. My once logical mind attempted to reject the object that stood dilapidated in front of me. Was I home? Was this my home so long ago? Confirmation came to me in the form of faded numbers on the now blackened panels of 4237 Berkshire Lane. The door hung open on one hinge as if wanting me to enter.

It happened – more or less – like this...

1957

Beatrice could not believe her luck. Out of all the girls at school, Brad Eggers asked her to the Eighth grade dance. She ran home that day, nearly dropping her books in the mud along the way. The smile that graced her young face was wider than any smile could ever be. She was in fact so happy that she hadn't noticed that she was skipping.

Brad Eggers, according to the school hallways and popularity seekers, was the cutest and most sought-after boy in school. He wore his sandy blonde hair slightly longer than what was acceptable, and Beatrice liked especially the way it curled just above his collar. He always wore the coolest clothes too. Not the nauseating leather jacket and jeans that seemed to be all the rage but nice clothes. Clothes that spoke of his intelligence; crisp white shirts tucked tightly into black denim. He didn't always need to dress up. Sometimes he would wear jeans, but when he did, he just seemed to wear it better than the other boys. At the pinnacle of his appearance – according to Beatrice – were his eyes; blue as the ocean on some days and then bright as the sky on others.

Bradly – as Beatrice enjoys calling him – is also an athlete: basketball, baseball, and Beatrice's favorite sport, football. She would always go to all of his games, even before he knew that she even existed. Yes, Brad Eggers was quite the catch, and with the proper amount of cunning and courage, Beatrice had managed to reel him in.

It happened – more or less – like this…

During first period homeroom, Rhonda Jennings asked Beatrice if she had found a date for the dance yet. Beatrice quietly shook her head.

"The dance is this Friday, Bea," Rhonda told her. "What are you gonna do?"

What she meant was 'who are you going to ask?' but it wasn't entirely proper for a girl to ask a boy. Those that did were taking a risk of being avoided like the plague for the rest of the school year, if not longer. Middle school etiquette dictated that the boy must ask the girl a week in advance of the event. If more time were provided, the girl might be given an opportunity to change her mind and go with someone else. If less time is given, say three days' notice, the boy will not have any time to change his mind. No, a week was the agreed upon time frame. The problem here was the dance was on Friday and it was Tuesday. The day before, Bobby Wilkins had asked Rhonda, so her worries were over as far as the dance was concerned.

Beatrice looked around the room with hopeful dismay in her watery green eyes, searching for that one boy that she knew had not yet asked anyone. She saw Matt Campbell, nope. Trevor Heath? Nope. Danny Ginsburg? Not on your life. To her left at the one o'clock position was Joe Stapleton. He was cute. She had a crush on him in Sixth grade but never acted on it. She knew that he had asked Kristi Burk, but it was the boy sitting next to Joe Stapleton that caught her eye. Yes, it was the one and only Brad Eggers. If he had asked someone, Beatrice would know, or at least Rhonda would know then Beatrice would know. Actually, the whole school would know. As far as Beatrice was aware, Brad was available. So she inhaled deeply and garnered as much courage as one girl could muster.

“I’m doing it,” Beatrice said.

“Doing what?”

“I’m gonna go ask Brad.”

“Brad?” Rhonda was dumbfounded. “Brad who? Brad Eggers? No way? You’re gonna ask him?”

“I sure am. And I’m doing it right now.”

Rhonda watched as her best friend stood from her desk, straightened out her skirt, and stepped towards the back of the class. Her strides were long and steady; almost sultry. The smile on her face was braced with purposeful confidence. To Rhonda, it seemed more like hopeful ridiculousness. Beatrice crossed the distance in almost no time at all. Brad looked up to see her just before she tripped and fell, right on her butt. The entire class laughed; pointing and gawking at her misfortune. All except for Rhonda and Brad, the latter of the two rushing over to help her up.

"Are you alright, Beatrice?" he asked – offering his hand. "That was some fall."

Beatrice feigned light-headedness. She took his hand and beamed into his blue eyes. It was all she could do to keep her cheeks from flushing, but the bruised rump and slightly lacerated ego helped to alleviate that. She was also somewhat taken aback that he knew her name. Once she gained her balance and composure, she decided it was time to set the trap.

"Thanks," she told him. "Sorry, that was embarrassing."

"Actually, as falls go, that wasn't too bad."

"I think I may have twisted my ankle. Would you mind carrying my books to my locker?" She could feel Rhonda's eyes burning a hole through the back of her head as the boy agreed to help her. The bell rang and Beatrice limped over and retrieved her books, giving Rhonda a little wink in the process. Brad took them from her and escorted her to her locker, which, fortunately for Beatrice, was down the back side of the building. So, they walked together, her arm inside his for balance, and to keep up the pretense that she really had twisted her ankle. A fake limp was a small price to pay for the cutest boy in school.

Once at her locker, Beatrice squeezed his bicep as she put her books away and Brad was confronted with an onslaught of emotions as blood quickly rushed to his extremities.

“Doing anything this Friday?” Brad asked – his palms sweaty with nervous energy.

“Icing my foot, no doubt. Why? What are you doing?”

“Oh, well, I, um, I was thinking that you might want to go to the dance with me?”

“There’s a dance on Friday?” Coy Beatrice, very coy.

“Why yes. It’s the Eighth-grade dance.”

Beatrice's heart was on fire. But of course, she didn’t want to let on to Brad that she was completely over the moon at the idea. In a matter of milliseconds, she thought of what she would wear, the ribbon she would tie her hair back with. She might need to ask her mother for a new pair of shoes. Would she kiss him? Maybe.

“Yes.”

“What? Huh?” Bradly seemed stunned.

"Yes, Bradly. I'll go to the Eighth-grade dance with you."

Beatrice squeezed Bradly's hand and limped away without another word; leaving him alone at her locker to fight off the urge to smile.

Later that same evening, Beatrice was so elated about the upcoming dance that she was finding it difficult to fall asleep. She sat up for an hour before bedtime wondering how it would feel to have Bradly kiss her. Would he try? She hoped so. She had never kissed a boy before. She had thought about it several times but found no boy yet to be worthy of her heart. Bradly Eggers would be the winner.

She slipped lively out of bed and trod down to the kitchen for a cup of milk. She poured the milk and held it up to her mouth for a sip and stopped quickly. She heard whispering coming from the basement. No one was supposed to be down there without Father's permission so she immediately knew who it was: Bethany. She thought about catching her in whatever she was doing and then squealing to Dad. Bethany would do the same thing. But then she thought twice about it. As a matter of fact, Beatrice didn't care what her sister did. Back to bed, she thought. But as her mind twirled inside a torrent of curiosity, Beatrice was certain that she heard two voices whispering down there. This she had to see. Just a peek then she would go to sleep. If Beth had a boy in the house with her, this would be some juicy gossip.

At the bottom of the stairs, Beatrice saw a faint light coming from the far side of the basement; by Father's study. Boy, would she be in trouble if they found out. She crept closer, keeping to the shadows. The whispers were somewhat louder, though she was unable to discern what was being said. Closer she came until she was able to see Bethany and another person sitting on the old couch. It was a boy! Oh, my goodness, Beatrice thought to herself. Now she was in trouble. She would not be able or even willing to keep this hidden from their parents.

She dared herself to take another step closer; and she did, keeping to the shadows along the back wall. Then she heard a whisper, and a name: Bradly. Beatrice bristled with fear. Not fear of the dark or anything ghastly but for Beatrice, it was a far greater fear; the fear of humiliation. She heard the whispered name again and her bravado became incendiary. She bolted from the shadow and pulled the chain for the overhead light, washing all of them in a pale yellow haze. What Beatrice saw took her breath away. On the old torn couch were her sister Bethany and Bradly Eggers. their shoes were off, and her pants were unbuttoned. They were kissing – his hand was up her shirt.

Bradly looked up at Bethany, shocked. He had actually thought that he was making out with Beatrice. Beatrice stifled a sob. She would not give either of them the satisfaction. She simply smiled and pulled the chain and switched the light off. She walked proudly and sickly back to the stairs, but before she left, she turned around and said quietly:

"Have fun with her while you can, Brad. That's as close to me as you will ever get."

Bethany looked at Brad and smiled her favorite menacing grin.

"She's right."

Welcome home, Walter

My eyes continued to deceive me as I toiled about the broken home of my once happy childhood. Dishes still sat on the rotted wood of the dining table. My toys, strewn about the floor, resting where I last abandoned them decades prior. I strolled down the front hallway that led to the kitchen. Portraits of actors and actresses portraying members of a happy family adorned the yellowed walls of mold. Faces familiar yet unrecognizable, danced under glass and wood, infested with age.

Dust and rat feces clung to everything like horrid words on a dirty page, and in the midst of my exploration I stumbled upon a box sitting untouched on the parlor floor. Not as unusual as one might gather. Boxes seemed to be all about the floor in different stages of decay. Yet this box was altogether different. For one it was clean; devoid of dust and dirt. Not a single particle of misuse sat upon it. The box was of a dark wood manufacture, with a hint of red in the grain. Perhaps cherry or mahogany. It was stained to shimmering brilliance. So much so that I was startled to see my face as clear as a looking glass. My face, and yet not my face at all. Had I seen this box before? Remembrance was a foolish institution and I hastily shrugged off the feeling. Its hinges were brass. That much was obvious. Brass of the highest quality. I dared open it then thought against it. What the damned hell do I care about some box? And yet, it was placed in the middle of the parlor. On the dusty floor for anyone to see. Anyone? No, not anyone. Me. It had been placed there for me to find, hadn't it?

My mind was aware of something just out of my line of sight. Blackish and without shape. Like an early morning mist, or a fog upon a slow flowing river, only darker and more malevolent. My eyes would not see it, yet I knew it was there all the same, watching me as if it were collecting information. I lifted the box to examine the weight and instantly felt something shift from within. The black shape that was still just out of my sight moved closer. I could feel its foul breath upon my neck, and I turned. It retreated and slithered into a corner.

Holding the box with the utmost care, I lifted the hasp and

noticed that it was crafted in the shape of a boar's head. Once again, I felt the surge of something terrible and I shook my head to extinguish the cobwebs. The hand-crafted hinges groaned in complaint as I worked the lid open. I set the box back down onto the broken floorboards and stepped away in haste. One step, then another. I had backed into what remained of the kitchen table, ridden with termites and stumbled forward in surprise. The black shape fell upon me. I felt absorbed within it and I was forced against my will to view the contents of the box. At once, I was confused by what I beheld. Blood, fresh crimson blood. As I watched, the blood began to pool around the edges, sloshing like an unmanned boat, lost at sea. It spilled onto the floor and was absorbed into the moldy wooden floor. The old wood turned dark like the Red Sea and instantly the house quaked, and I swore to the saints that I heard it take a breath. It spoke to me. I trembled with abject fear.

What are you afraid of, Walter? Surely there is nothing for you to fear in this place.

"Whose blood is this?" I asked out loud as the trembling of the old home increased. I became unbalanced and lost my footing. An opening in the floor appeared like a gaping maw and I had the sense that it intended to swallow me whole. I reached out and grasped the leg of the oak sideboard that my mother had purchased, and it broke off and disintegrated in my hand like wet dust. I fell, my hands – red with blood – grabbed hold of the ancient flooring. The black malevolence appeared above me like a swirling ball of evil. I asked again.

"Whose blood is this? I demand you tell me!"

Why, it's your blood, Walter. The blood is yours.

A black hand of evil was placed upon my head and I fell into a pit of blackness. I cannot tell you how far or how long I fell; only that I fell. The void seemed endless – a bottomless pit where nothing existed yet evil resided for all eternity. I feared that I might fall forever, that this had now become my fate. There was nothing more to my life, only the falling. From above me, or below me – I can't be certain for my orientation was skewed from the falling – came a pale blue light; soft at first like moonlight reflected off of freshly fallen snow. The further I fell the brighter the light became, and I strained my arms to reach for it. I wanted to be near the light. I needed the light.

At once, and quite instinctively, I inhaled fresh air as if it were my very first breath. I felt about my body – checking for missing parts or broken limbs. I was whole and intact, but not of sound mind. I closed my eyes in a vain attempt to ward off the evil that the black shape fought to engulf me in. As I lost myself in sleep, I knew that my mind was behaving as it had only hours before.

A fire must be lit

I awoke with a shudder to a sound that I can only describe as sawing wood. And as my eyes adjusted to the glow effusing through the portiere, I was relieved at the realization that it had all been a dream. I was safe at home, in bed – worrying about nothing more than the unrelenting din of life from down upon Herald Circle. I smiled with childlike mirth on the occasion. Summer had finally arrived. I stepped onto the cold oak floor to retrieve a match from the mantle. T'was still early. A chill from the night lingered and a fire must be lit. With a loving posture, I kissed my mother's picture and opened the flue. A curtain of dust-filled sunlight caressed the wood floor and I halted. Something was amiss. Perhaps my mind was having its way with me, or maybe this was a residue leftover from the previous night's horrible dream, but I had always known sunlight to be golden yellow. Yet the glow of light radiating through my bedroom window was a fiery burnt orange.

The clock on the mantle read 7:32 AM. I quickly ran to my

night table to reference my wristwatch. The time was accurate. I stood staunchly before the window with my hand upon the draperies. My body went cold as I pulled the curtain apart and spied the scene below. I gasped in horror. The world as I knew it, or as I had once come to know it, was gone. In its place was an inferno. A blazing mass of fire. The library on the corner of Wilshire and Primrose was engulfed in flames as large as the building itself. The market where I was to purchase my rice for this evening's supper was no more; a pile of red and white embers infused with soot black as night. The park, my beautiful park was all but gone.

I quickly thought of the helpless people that might have been caught in this hell on earth but noticed almost instantly that there was an odd lack of movement. Where was everyone? Where were the sirens, the emergency crews? Why was there no effort being put forth to stop the blaze? The only vehicles in view were those left abandoned on the street – gutted by fire.

Walter, get a grip on yourself.

I spun on my heels to face my bedroom door. The voice had come from that direction. Cautiously I stepped into my chamber to have a look. All was quiet. And yet I noticed that the drapes had been pushed aside. This was an impossibility. The drapes in my room are never opened for any reason. I like it dark when I sleep, so dark that I couldn't see my hand in front of my own face. It's a quirk, I know, but let's move along. I inserted myself back into the parlor. The room had gone cold and turned a dark gray like the color of a winter evening. The room itself felt smaller and the fire that I had only recently lit had gone out without even a memory. My heart began to palpitate, and I reached for the glass of water sitting innocently unaware on my night table. The voice that I had heard was the same. The same from my dream. My nightmare. I placed the glass onto the sill and turned back to the horror below. What will become of me now? I thought. All that I know is gone. Was I to loiter about the world alone?

I wiped my mouth with the sleeve of my nightshirt and regained my composure. Absurd. My rationale had returned in earnest and I moved with haste to my wardrobe. I must go down and help whoever I can. I dressed for the occasion, as I always do: jeans and my new white Provatchi t-shirt. One must look dashing even during the worst of situations. And if the world was coming to an end then I was certainly going to look my best. While lacing my boots I stole one last glance out my window. There, in the middle of the westbound side of Sweetwater, was a child. And if my eyes did not deceive me, it was a girl. I was guessing of course but she appeared to me to be no older than seven or eight. I put the laces in God's hands and ran down the stairs and burst through the front door and out into the heat of purgatory.

Down on the street my boots fell upon an endless beach of broken glass and debris. I was horrified to see the charred remains of so many of my neighbors, there on the street before me. The smell of rot covered my once beautiful city, and at once I turned around to see my own building engulfed in flame; the windows broken, shutters turned to ash. The very front door that I had just exited was in black pieces upon the steps themselves. But I had no time to ponder. I turned east down Herald Circle and quickly turned left onto Sweetwater. The girl was there, just as I had seen her from my bedroom window and I was forced to look back upon my apartment that was no longer standing. Her dress was blue like the sky once was. There was a ribbon of white silk holding ruby red curls in place. White stockings were worn underneath shoes of shiny black. She had her back turned to me as I approached.

"Walter," she said – her back still turned.

I came closer and asked her if she was alright and where her parents might be. I would be more than happy to help her to find them.

"Walter." The sound was that of a whisper yet vociferous in my ears.

Her Face

The flames from the surrounding neighborhood threw intense heat on my face as I circled her. I stood, yes, but my legs felt as if they were no longer holding me erect. I must say now that it is quite arduous and painful to describe what I saw once I faced her. Her hair, once bouncy with curls, was dirty with soot and matted to her face. Her dress was burned and fell in rags off her shoulders. The skin of her limbs was blistered and broken, puss oozed from open wounds. Her face was a mask of death. Charred pieces of flesh hung off of her face like torn meat. There was a gash that ran from her chin down to the top of her neck, open and black with dried blood. Her nose was flat as if she had fallen directly on it. The eyes – no, I cannot speak of her eyes for she had none. In their place were two black marbles – lidless – that dripped down her burnt cheeks as if they were melting from the intense heat. When she opened her mouth, her teeth appeared to match the color of the surrounding devastation. Her breath was that of rotting flesh.

She raised her arms and it was then that I saw that in her hands she held a box. I gasped at the sight of that box. Yes, the same box from my dream of the night before. The same glossy red finish. The same boar's head clasp, with hinges made of brass. She held it aloft towards me – urging me without words to take it from her. I resisted.

"Walter." My name, issued from her, but not her mouth, set my skin to chill.

Without warning or fanfare, the box opened of its own purpose and I felt the earth tremble under my feet. Fire rained upon the ground from a burning sky. I had expected to see the same thick crimson blood that was my own, but I was momentarily relieved when the box appeared to hold nothing at all. The girl held the box higher, willing me to relieve her of it. Reluctantly I did. And upon doing so, the girl transformed. Gone were the charred pieces of hanging flesh. Black, lifeless eyes were replaced by eyes as green as a meadow. Her hair was a dark red, bordering on mahogany, and when she smiled the sun reflected off of her pretty face. She had changed, but she was no longer the little girl that I had seen, that I had spoken to and taken the box from. As if some sort of magic or trickery was taking place, the girl was now a beautiful young woman, easily the age of thirty five. She was tall and slim, but not too slim. Athletic, yes, that's more like it.

I had forgotten about the cursed box I was holding and continued to stare at her. The holocaust that had taken over the city was now gone. The colors of summer had returned and all around me was life. The sound of children rang throughout the streets and shop owners turned their welcome signs to 'Open'. Cars and buses drove past me as I stood still, in the middle of Sweetwater Drive, as she lifted her hand to touch my face.

"Do I know you?' I asked. She didn't speak. A nod of her head and a smile was her answer. "How do I know you?" Again, she did not answer or refused to answer, I'm not sure of which. She held my face and my gaze and smiled a smile of the heart. The smile of an innocent child on a snowy Christmas morning. I noticed a silver bracelet on her wrist as she touched my face. It was small and inexpensive but with an inscription that read "To Beatrice" and knew right there who she was.

I hate you

1960

"Rodney!" Beatrice yelled. Her and Rhonda had been walking up and down all the streets and drives and avenues of the neighborhood – searching. It was a desperate search, one that required more than just the two of them. Earlier that morning, Beatrice's dog Rodney had jumped the fence and ran off. He had never run away before so they had hoped that he was somewhere close but, after two hours of searching, her hope was fading. Beatrice loved that dog. She'd raised him from a puppy.

Beatrice met little Rodney on her tenth birthday when her father pulled up from being late at work. The snow was falling hard but everyone in the house watched as he pulled a box from the back seat and hefted it up to the door. Beatrice couldn't hold her patience so she opened the door quickly to let her father in. Beatrice jumped at the box, but her father held fast.

"Oh, just give her the damn thing so she'll shut up," Bethany said from the top of the stairs.

"Don't be cross, Bethany," their father told her. "This is for you as well."

But, as usual, Bethany wanted nothing to do with her birthday or a birthday party. She laughed and stormed up to her room and slammed the door.

Beatrice could wait no longer. Her father set the box down on the floor and Beatrice attacked it like a lioness. There was no wrapping, but the box was sealed with tape. Just as she was able to relieve one side of it, a tiny wet nose popped out. Beatrice squealed. She yanked open the top and saw a puppy with bright orange fur and big, dark eyes. The puppy quickly jumped into her arms and licked her face excitedly.

"Can I name him, Daddy, please? Can I?"

"Of course, Beatrice. He's yours," her father said, then looked up the stairs. "Yours and Bethany's." Beatrice ran to the bottom of the stairs.

"Beth, come see what we got. Please? He's for you and me!" But the bedroom door didn't open. Bethany would not see the joy that one little dog had given to her.

"Rodney!" she called happily. "His name is Rodney."

"Why Rodney, little one?"

"I don't know. He just looks like a Rodney."

"Rodney! Come here, boy!"

The two girls continued to blanket the entire neighborhood, going house to house, searching backyards, woods, playgrounds, and anywhere a dog might be hiding. The neighborhood kids came out of their houses and took on the search with them. To Beatrice, this was a hopeful turn of events. More boots on the ground meant that they could cover a larger area in a shorter time. Together, the kids came up with a plan. Beatrice and Rhonda would scour Berkshire to Palmer. Brent and Judy, with their dog Roxy, would take Sheridan down to Winfield, while Nancy and Patricia took the entire length of Liberty street. In three hours they would all meet back at Beatrice's house. While all of this searching was going on, Mr. Kleinfeldt and his youngest child, Mark, drove around town handing out flyers that Beatrice had drawn that morning. Mrs. Kleinfeldt stayed at home making phone calls to friends that might be outside the search area. A valiant effort has never been seen before or since – all in vain.

Rodney was nowhere to be found, and Beatrice sat at the kitchen table and cried, her lap full of flyers. At the same moment, Bethany entered the kitchen with a smirk on her face and opened the refrigerator. Mark ran through holding a small teddy bear. Bethany scooped him up and whispered in his ear. After which, she placed him back down. Little Mark then smiled and ran to the window facing the back yard and pointed.

"Mommy, Mommy, look it!" the boy exclaimed. Mrs. Kleinfeldt came to the window and lifted up her son. She kissed him eagerly and followed his little finger to the large elm tree in the back yard. A terrified scream escaped from her mouth and she put the boy down, hurrying to her husband, sitting in the living room.

Mr. Kleinfeldt instructed them all to stay inside the house then walked around to the back yard. At the end of the patio, he halted. His face went white as he viewed the horror only fifty feet away. Hanging from a branch of the elm tree, attached to what appeared to him to be an actual noose, was Rodney. His eyes were open and his tongue hanging from his mouth. He had been cut open from his jaw to his belly and the blood had gathered in a pool on the ground beneath him. He ran to the tree and frantically cut the dog down. From inside the house, he could hear the cries of anguish from those watching, especially Beatrice. His heart broke for her as he carried the dog to the side of the house. He retrieved a shovel from the garage and quickly set to burying the poor animal.

Back inside, Beatrice became hysterical. She ran to the door – wanting to stop her father from burying her dog; not believing that he was dead. Her mother held her, trying her best to comfort her. Carrying a small carton of milk, Bethany walked past them.

"Who cares about some stupid dog?"

"Bethany!" her mother yelled. "March up to your room, young lady."

"Gladly."

"I know it was you, Beth." Beatrice snarled. Bethany stopped at the middle of the staircase – not turning around. "You hated Rodney. You always did. You hate everything. And now, I hate you. You're not my sister anymore. Don't look at me. Don't talk to me. Don't even think about me."

Bethany smiled. Killing the dog had the effect she was hoping for. Her goal in life was to take away everything that Beatrice loved. Nothing in life gave her more joy than seeing her sister cry.

"What are you doing here?"

"Mom?" It was the only word that I could say. Again, she nodded her head – unable to speak. "What are you doing here?" She pointed at the box that I held and stepped back to leave. I wanted to ask her how she was: what was it like there? I wanted to know why she had to die. I wanted to tell her about all the nights that I lay awake dreaming of all the times she sang to me; that it made me feel safe and protected before the darkness changed her and the bottle took her. I wanted to tell her that I loved her and miss her so very much. But most of all I wanted to say thank you; Thank you, Mom. Thank you for my life. I wanted all these things, but she just kept pointing at the box as she faded into a soft blue mist.

If I seemed at the time to be somewhat apprehensive, it may have been because I was standing in the middle of the busiest street in the city, holding a box that once held my blood, given to me by my Mother who had been long dead. Once on the sidewalk and out of harm's way, I looked again at the life around me. I felt my cheek and could still smell my mother's hand upon me. The strong scent of lilac gathered there. I breathed a well-earned sigh of relief. And it was then that I saw the box. I had placed it down on the concrete after reaching the side of the road. I could see the window of my apartment from where I stood, and I felt comforted that I was okay, and that I was going to be okay, and that the world was okay. So, I lifted the box. It had closed after the dead girl had given it to me. A quick glimpse of fire in my mind held me fast and within a second it was gone. I carefully lifted the clasp and opened the box. The hinges once again protesting my involvement. To my surprise, the box was not empty. Though it did not hold the gore that was in my dream, I still remained on guard. Inside the box, resting on soft, red velvet, was a folded piece of torn notebook paper; like a note passed in English class to the girl you want to take to the dance. I retrieved the note and placed the box carefully on the grass. With this, the air around became like ice. The colors of my long-awaited summer were gone, replaced by gray and black. The fire of hell had not returned but this was just as sinister. There was a hideous growl from behind me and the ground again shook under my feet. Cold breath expelled visibly into vapor from my mouth as I unfolded the paper to read one word written in still wet red ink.

Run!

Run!

I was never one to not obey an order given to me from my mother.

I ran. In the direction of the sun. Just the simple fact that it was once again shining was a smart enough direction for me to take. I ran hard and fast. So hard that my hands began to shake, and my breathing became labored. I was acquainted with this feeling. Oftentimes, on my bicycle, I would ride longer than needed; to eliminate the unwanted body mass of course. The pain in my side made it worse but it didn't stop me from running. Not too long after I began, I once again became unfamiliar with my surroundings. I knew not of where I was. This was maddening because I was not but only three of four blocks from home. The houses here were old. Not run-down and neglected but historic. In contrast, they appeared new. The owners of these historic old homes took quite a bit of care of them. It was refreshing to see. More often than not, older neighborhoods are abandoned and left to dust, or worse yet, taken over by street thugs and ruffians, so I was surprised to see that not a one had been left to rot.

I ran; turning left and then right, down streets and avenues; circles and places; roads and boulevards. The blur of life passing unnoticed. If I had noticed, or even cared, would I have seen the automobiles that lined these streets? Would I have seen that they were from a period that was not in the present? My memory hadn't punctuated this until later that evening when I realized that the entire neighborhood was a still-life from the 1920's. In the moment though, I was far too concerned with my own safety. My fear was telling me to keep running.

I ran; still holding my side, into a rickety termite infested covered bridge. Here was where I stopped to breathe. I heard the clip-clop of horses, though none were around. The echo of a broken calliope, its intonation no longer true, bounced off the wooden planks and I was instantly unnerved. I felt the notion that I was being watched from either ahead or behind. A dirty creek ran fast under the bridge and I heard the wind blow a clean b flat through a bank of reeds somewhere near the edge of the creek. It was as if I were sitting restlessly in a movie theater, watching a film that I had never heard anything about, with actors I knew nothing of, about a guy no one gave a shit about. It was an odd feeling.

Then, from somewhere up ahead, the sound of a saxophone pierced the late afternoon and I decided to put my feet to moving once again.

At its end, the bridge opened upon a village full of lustrous life. The colors of summer were bold and intoxicating. Children rode bicycles in packs while couples held hands – strolling down a lane of such color and beauty. Throngs of people converged upon single spot up ahead. I joined them. The point of interest was a stage, with chairs placed around it. A brass band of children from the local high school sat in their uniforms, their instruments in their laps, listening to the speaker standing behind a podium. The man behind the podium was tall, over six feet by my estimation. He was speaking enthusiastically while a group of people sat on the stage behind him. A banner above the stage announced that it was the 25th annual Daisy Festival.

"My fellow citizens!" He went on and on about prosperity and the future and all that. I wasn't really listening. I stood to the right of the stage next to a hydrant that was leaking. An unleashed Jack Russell sat and allowed the water to trickle into its open mouth. A young girl seated in the second row was staring at me like she knew who I was. She was attractive. No, that's not true at all. She was beyond attractive. She was beautiful. I'm not even certain that beautiful is the correct word either. She wore a white summer dress – colored with pink and yellow flowers. Her hair was black – shoulder length and placed behind her delicate ears. Her skin was pale, but not alarmingly so. Her eyes were what caught my attention; and my breath. You could say by seeing them that they were blue but only technically. Icy-blue and gray splattered with flecks of silver – the color of frozen mercury. I couldn't take my eyes off her.

She smiled and showed a luscious mouthful of perfectly straight, gleaming white teeth. My pulse quickened and I found that I was making a spectacle of myself. I was having visions that there was no way possible to control. Visions of this young woman and I doing things that made it difficult for me to remain standing there in public. A feeling of nausea rose from my belly. Somehow, she was doing this to me. The visions started innocent enough. The sex, though sometimes rough and aggressive, was nothing short of exciting. But then there was blood. The blood wasn't mine; it was hers and I was forced to drink it. She introduced more partners into our love making. This act would be considered normal if the additions were human. There were goats and dogs, a pig and a horse. The young lady began to speak a strange language and horns grew from her forehead. She grinned mischievously at this and a drop of blood fell from the corner of her lips.

I protested but was unable to remove the images from my mind, as if they were really happening. With a flash, they were gone, and I heard the tall man speaking again. The woman, still staring at me, smiled and licked a bloody finger. I stepped back in fear. Where the hell was I? My stride lengthened and I found myself back under the safety of the covered bridge. Before I realized what was happening, I was running again – this time faster than before, with a greater purpose.

Within a small amount of time, I was home. I found my car in the parking garage where I left it and jumped in. My heart was still racing from the horrific imagery my mind was unable to escape from.

Debra

I drove hard. Perhaps a little too hard given the posted speed limits but I was unconcerned. Ironically there was no other living soul on the road for me to be disconcerted with. I needed to remove myself from everything familiar. Which included removing myself from myself, if that makes any sense at all. I had even considered subletting my apartment for a few months to one of those out-of-town types; what are they called? Airbnb? But the idea of a stranger and his germ-laden lady friend rubbing their genitals across my bathroom tile left me with hives. So, I packed as much as I could hold in the back seat, made a worthwhile withdrawal, and put the rubber to the road. Where was I heading? I did not know. I had no more inclination than you, my dear friend. Family was out of the question. Most of them were dead. Uncle Rupert had always made me feel uncomfortable; like I was in constant need to empty my bladder. I did have two cousins on my Mother's side that were always entertaining, but spending the summer in a two bedroom, playing video games with a constant pizza contact high did not appeal to me. No, I was to be alone. And if I was to be alone, I wanted to be alone without the concern of friends and the mindless pop-ins from well-wishing distant family members.

An investigation needed to be launched. I needed to find someone that might assist me in learning just what in God's name is wrong with me. Is it a physician I require? Perhaps I simply need to talk with someone – a professional. Am I crazy? Am I talking about visiting a psychiatrist? Dear Lord, save me. I've never put too much stock in their kind. Back in college, a girlfriend had suggested that, because I'm not much of a romantic, we should seek couples' therapy. I responded to her suggestion by leaving her a Post-it suggesting that she never call me again. Reasonable, don't you think? Are these visions dreams or are they real? Call me mad but they feel as real as the wind on my face. And yet I am unaware of anyone by the name of Penelope. The little memory I have of her is fleeting. But I could feel her – taste her. I smelled her on my skin. So many questions needed answering. If it had all been a dream, why was I coveting a pearl – the single pearl that I pocketed in Randolph's? If there were no Penelope, how had I come about the pearl? And what of that box, that terrible box that seems to be at the center of my nightmares? Nightmares that aren't actually nightmares but visions. I cannot wrap my mind around its appearance. Nor can I resolve the notion that I am still – though driving – walking through a dream; a trance-like existence that I am unable to return from. Where will I end up next?

After two hours of arrow-straight blacktop, I involuntarily took the first exit I came to, not realizing at the time that I had turned off the highway at Route 83 towards Middleton. Typical. No matter how strong I felt or how staunch my will power had developed over the years, I could never erase the memories of Debra. Even now I cannot explain why I turned towards her home, towards her. It's possible that I believed she could help me. I needed to talk to someone and Debra was who I needed. She was my rock. Yes, she currently holds a hatred towards me that can only be described as complicated, but Debra was always kind. Smart and kind. And loyal. We had known each other since we were children – friendship being more important than annoying intimacy. During high school, our bond became stronger as we realized that we were spending more time together than most married couples do. The sex had been her idea. I still believe it was a mistake but Debra insisted that we do; if only, she said, as a test – to see if we could handle the mental rigors of being intimate with your best friend. In her mind, the test was a success, and we began having sex on a regular basis. When I say regular, I mean every day of the week. Sometimes as much as three times in one single twenty-four-hour period.

After high school, I was relieved to learn that she would not be following me to college. I chose UCLA on purpose. Not only because I wasn't accepted to Harvard Law, but because it was far enough away from everything I wanted to be free from. I had no family to keep me close to home so it made sense to leave. But as the months went by, I missed Debra, and I told her so often – in phone calls and letters. Then during Christmas break of my freshmen year, Debra flew out to visit me. What started out as a two-week visit became a six-month love affair that neither of us were really prepared for, if you ask me. We loved with our bodies and our hearts. We were inseparable; joined at the hip as it were. I moved out of the dorm and we rented an apartment on campus together. We were happy. But as you know, happiness is temporary and is only achieved when both parties are satisfied. She was. I was not.

After the spring semester let out and I came home, Debra and I tried again to make it work, but it was hard; too hard for both of us for it to be worth the struggle.

So, here I was, about to see her once again. If I could only remember the way to her flat. But what would I say? How could I possibly explain any of this madness? I didn't believe it; how could I expect anyone else to?

The apartment building was as I remembered it; red brick and boring as hell. The interior was cozy enough if not slightly claustrophobic. I briskly took the path to the door, taking notice of the cars in the lot, not remembering what she was currently driving. Didn't she drive a Bug at one time? An older gentleman in a black wool Peacoat with a white scarf and muddy fishing boots stood near the door as I pressed the buzzer to apt 3B. My first impression was that he was waiting for a friend to come down from one of the many dwellings, but obviously, he was out of his mind. A wool Peacoat – in July? It was well past 9 PM and it was close to 85 degrees. I tried not to stare but my impulse got the best of me.

"You must be burning up in that coat, friend."

He opened his mouth to speak and I was instantly repulsed by the state of his oral hygiene. The man had no teeth, and there were what looked like sores all throughout his gums. Uncomfortable, I pressed the button again and put a greater space between him and me.

I spotted a shadow move from the stairwell through the glass door and I hoped that Deb was making her way to the door. She would let me in and listen to me. She would put out some wine and a plate of olives. Of course, an explanation on my part would most certainly be required. Would she understand? I believe she would. Debra was always a kind sort, even after she found me passed out drunk with another woman. That other woman is her best friend Holly. Fortunately, or perhaps, unfortunately, the memory of that evening haunts me still, suffice it to say that I had, at the time, wished I had been sober.

The longer I stood there next to that man, the greater his stench became. Trust me when I say that he was foul smelling. His long silver-black hair was greasy and matted to his face and, I'm not entirely sure, but it looked like there were earthworms within it.

A hum and a buzz erupted from the glass door and I pulled it open – glancing back at the Peacoat clad fool to hold the door open for him but he had vanished. I shrugged then entered.

On the third floor, I found my sweet Debra waiting for me just beyond the transom, her door open. She said nothing as I walked in and slipped off my shoes.

"I never dreamed that this day would come, Walter," she said, pouring us both a glass of cheap wine. Told you. "I was never worried about seeing you at the mall or stuck at a stoplight. Incidental sightings would be just an occupational hazard. But I never thought that you would actually be here, ringing my doorbell. I had written you off. It took me a while but I got over you. So, you can see how your appearance at my door is a bit of a puzzle."

I told her about my journey west, the subliminal exit. Not knowing myself why I had come. I told her of the foul-breathed man waiting outside her building. But I saved the best for last.

"I think I'm going crazy." I ran my fingers over my sweaty scalp. "I've been having some very odd dreams lately, Debra. More often than not they feel just as real as any other time that I'm awake." She sat across from me on a leather divan, her cat napping at her feet. "The dreams have become more and more horrific that I am questioning my own sanity. You know that I put no stock in anything paranormal, but I remember that you were into that stuff." I sighed heavily and my head sank into my chest. From the divan, I heard a snicker and looked up to see her smiling.

"Well, look at you now," she said loudly, standing up. "Wasn't it you that told me, all those years ago, that you were immune to emotional problems?"

"Yes."

"And wasn't it you that said, 'Anyone who sees a psychiatrist on a regular basis is wasting their money'?"

"Yes."

"And here you are; Walter Kirk, of all people, sitting on my couch, telling me that it's you that's going crazy. When it wasn't more than seven years ago that you criticized me for seeing a therapist. Not a psychiatrist, or a psychologist, Walter, but a therapist; a counselor. Simply because I was having trouble dealing with my brother's suicide. Do you remember what you said to me the day after his funeral?" I did but I was not going to allow her to use it against me, so I said nothing. "I'll refresh your memory. 'You'll be fine my dear. You just need to move on.'" Yes, I said those very words but, allow me to assure you that they have been taken out of context. Her emotional breakdown was affecting her physically. She was unable to work, or even perform the most basic human functions. I just wanted her to live, to take hold of her life.

She was pacing through the entire apartment. Stopping here, turning around, walking there, turning around. She would pick up the television remote and turn the volume down then all at once change her mind. Stepping into the kitchen, she drained her glass and poured herself another then continued pacing again. The cat watched her anxiously from the carpeted floor. When she passed in front of the small bookshelf that she had purchased at a second-hand store, she would pick out a book; a heavy one. I was afraid that if she found the right one, she would fling it through the air at me. She was a strange bird, my Debra, but I needed her to understand. No, I needed her to listen. She was standing in front of the patio door now, its sliding door open to the arid breeze outside, and for a moment, I thought that I had heard someone talking. My attention was pulled from Debra for the smallest moment – like a dog that suddenly sees a squirrel. Of course, I heard someone talking. I'm such an imbecile. Debra is not alone in this building. Certainly, there are others with their patio doors open as well. The voices were muffled but aggressive – male if I had to guess. The conversation rose in volume, and the last word spoken was Walter. Seamlessly I forced my attention back to the situation at hand; in mid-sentence mind you.

"– the black mold. You remember that don't you? Then you remember who had to clean it up. I was always having to clean up after you. No, you weren't a messy person – not physically anyway. You had baggage. That's it. You had baggage, Walter. If it wasn't your car, it was your job, or James was on another date, or maybe your neighbor down the hall needed her garbage taken out every single day of her godforsaken life! And the countless hours spent on conversations about your mother. Wasn't it your turn to move on? I was always there for you but my God, Walter, when was it ever going to be my turn? When were you ever going to take my feelings into account?"

She was right. I'll be dammed if she wasn't right. I put my glass down on the cheap cork coaster resting sadly on the coffee table next to the linen scented candle and stood. Time to be a man. I ran the maze of tables and pillows standing in my way and I went to her; along the way, I ticked the boxes of necessary things that I needed to say to her. I stopped. She was leaning against the refrigerator with her glass resting precariously against her forehead. I placed my hand on her cheek and looked at her like a lover would. Her skin was just as soft as I remembered. Her eyes had the same effect that they did back in high school. She smiled and placed her hand over mine – a strong gesture.

"I'm sorry." For all the times I was wrong. For all the times I was right. For not being there when you needed me yet wanting you to be there for me. For the times I pushed you away, not needing your help. For all the times that I worked late and forgot to tell you that I was going out afterward. For all the times that I didn't accept you as you were; wanting you to change. For the time I accidentally killed your cat Rufus and allowed you to think that he merely escaped from the balcony. I'm sorry for not accepting that you didn't care for southern cuisine simply because of the amount of salt used, which, if you really consider it, is kind of silly. Anyway... I'm sorry that I bought a car instead of an engagement ring. I am very sorry for all these things that I can't bring myself to say. But mostly, I'm sorry for Judith; your other best friend. I had been drunk, and she more than I. "I'm very sorry, Debra."

She set her glass down on the kitchen counter and held my hand to her lips and kissed my fingers. One by one she put each of them in her mouth, imitating her favorite sex act. She smiled innocently and devilishly at the same time and I felt the blood rush in my veins like a sports car. I wanted to kiss her but I knew that it would be a mistake. I wanted her but I didn't want to lead her on. Every cell in my body told me to take her, to mount her right there on the kitchen floor. That's what she wants isn't it? It's what I wanted. But I couldn't do it. Perhaps if she were slightly less fragile, I might be more inclined to enter her.

Out of nowhere, a sound like broken concrete came from outside the building and Debra jumped.

Walter

I turned my face towards the front door where I swore I had heard a man's voice. Was it a man's voice? Was it the same voice that I had heard earlier? I was certain that I heard someone saying my name.

Walter

There it was again but Debra appeared unmoved by it. She wasn't hearing it. She was clutching at herself like a caged lioness who had been unloved for the longest time. I heard it. It wasn't loud, only a whisper, like that of the ragged girl, or a radio station, not exactly in tune. Were they now following me? They had to be following me. I was sure of it. But who were they? Have I no place left to go? From my pocket, I felt the hum of my cell and quickly pulled it out. Debra sighed. The same old Walter Kirk. The number was unfamiliar to me but I felt compelled to answer. She flopped onto the sofa and placed her hand down her pants, no longer amused with pleasuring me.

"Hello?"

"Walter!!!"

"James?" My college roommate.

"Walter! You have to help me!"

"Help you? With what? Another concubine? Is this one passed out as well?" I winked at Debra slyly. She rolled her eyes and turned the volume up on the television to drown out the uninteresting conversation. There was a rustling on the line and another man spoke. Maybe it wasn't another man but James disguising his voice. I'm not an expert on foreign languages but I was positive that it was German. Meanwhile, Debra began to tremble visibly. She appeared sickly and I moved out of the way in case she needed to vomit.

"Walter!!! He – "

The line went dead and I quickly redialed the number. No answer. No connection. No voicemail, nothing.

Walter

This time the voice sounded like it was in the room with me, whispering in my ear, tugging on my shirt sleeve. I was going mad. I turned toward the sitting area and saw Debra, still alone on the couch, no longer masturbating or trembling; a carving knife plunged deep into her skull. A single drop of blood creating a red line of gore from the wound to her mouth. Screaming, I spun back to the kitchen and she was still there, holding the empty glass of wine. She winked at me with devious eyes and I saw something I had never seen before from my sweet Debra. Her teeth looked broken. Not altogether rotted but jagged or sharpened. Her eyes were bloodshot and her hair was different – like it wasn't hers, cut or chopped at odd angles. She licked her lips and began to undress as she walked slowly from the kitchen to the bedroom. My body convulsed and I could feel myself falling into a void. No!!! I shouted – out loud, I think. If it makes any difference to you, I was under the assumption that the scene being played out before me was another hallucination; a horrific singularity from which I would eventually wake up from. A single blink proved I was correct. Debra was there, right where she was when I had answered the call from James.

"James!" I yelled.

"What about him?" Debra asked.

"I believe he's in trouble. That was him on the phone."

"The phone? When were you on the phone?"

"Just now. I was just talking to him when you – "

"When I what?"

"I am dreadfully sorry, Debra. I shouldn't have come here. I may have put you in danger." I backed away in the direction of the front door and Debra stood and rushed me. She seemed to be in a rage. Her now gnarled hands were upon my throat within seconds.

Her breath smelled of sulfur.

"Don't you dare fucking leave, you dirty son of a bitch! I own you now. You leave; you walk out that door and I will hunt you down like an animal and I will rip your intestines out through your mouth and feed them to my fucking dog. You understand me, cocksucker?" Upon that last word, her voice changed to a growl. It was guttural and terrifying. I opened the door slowly and stepped into the hallway – backing directly into the foul-smelling man that had been previously outside the building. The one difference was that this time he sported a black felt top hat. A terrifying look to be sure. Again, I screamed and the man opened his mouth as wide as an Illinois bass. Oddly, with his mouth disgustingly widened, his tongue blackened and charred, a whisper was uttered.

Walter.

Right then and there I should've run. I should've run down the stairs two at a time and burst through the glass door not giving a shit if it shattered. I should've jumped into the car and left. But I didn't. I turned once again to face Debra. She was standing rigidly in the doorway of her apartment, the same carving knife protruding from her forehead just above her right eye. She was naked and damaged, like a body long since dead. There was a fresh hole on the side of her face, full of maggots. In her hands, she held a box. An odd-looking jewelry box made of wood and stained red. The lid was flat and hinged in polished brass. The clasp was unnerving, to be honest. It was tooled in the shape of a pig. Wait, I know this box!

My mind fell upon a fading memory. The box. I had seen it before, hadn't I? Hadn't I been in this situation before? This same box – with, no… With my blood being held inside. But where and when I don't recall. It mattered not. I took the cursed box from Debra's dead hands and smashed it against the smelly man's head. A roar erupted from him that I cannot and will not describe to you.

This time, I did run. Unfortunately, the glass door refused to shatter as I ran through it. I had an unsettling feeling that my car wouldn't be there, but luckily I had never been so happy to be wrong in my life. I had left the top down and I jumped in like Steve McQueen running from the Gestapo. Nervously, I inserted the key and the engine roared like a lover on fire. And just like that, I was headed back home.

Where's my baby?

1970

Rain battered the steel reinforced windows of an already chaotic hospital room. The cinder block walls were unadorned and painted an annoying cream. The young woman in the small bed screamed in pain as a doctor and a nurse tended to her. Lightning struck not too far from the hospital and the lights flickered but held. It was late; 2:30 AM. The woman had checked herself in yesterday lunchtime, alone, stating that she was pregnant and that her water had broken. The delivery had been difficult, with hours upon hours of ceaseless anguish. Pain raked her body and she writhed in agony. She had been given medication for the pain but it wasn't working. A machine near her bed indicated that her blood pressure was dropping as the doctor worked quickly on the young mother. Thunder continued to erupt, shaking the windows. Nurses moved in and out of the cramped room as they cared for the child that they had just pulled from her.

The young woman watched frantically while one nurse came in and another would leave. She could not see or hear her baby. She didn't know if it was in the room or if it had been taken. She didn't even know if it was a boy or girl and, while her own trauma was being tended to, she desperately searched for a sign – any sign that would tell her that her baby was alright. After her stitches were in place and bandaged, she was given a shot; a pain reliever she was told.

"Where's my baby?" she asked

"He's being cared for," an overweight nurse explained. "The doctor will be back in shortly to explain."

"He? Are you telling me my baby is a boy?

"Get some rest, miss, you're going to need it."

The nurse closed the door behind her then ran to join the team in the Neonatal Intensive Care Unit. Upon delivery, the baby was in respiratory distress and was put on a ventilator. To make matters worse, the baby's heart was only functioning at thirty five percent. The pediatric surgeon was called immediately.

At 7:45 AM a tall, young doctor with wavy blonde hair and wire-rimmed glasses entered the mother's room with a nurse. He checked IV lines and made notes on a clipboard. The nurse opened the curtains and a blast of sunlight filled the room. The young woman woke and sought the doctor's eyes.

"When can I see my baby?" she pleaded with him. He referenced the chart one last time. The nurse was ready with a syringe.

"Miss Kleinfeldt... Bethany. Your baby was born with RSV; Respiratory Syncytial Virus, which caused his little lungs to fill with fluid. This also caused his heart to work harder than it was able to. We held him on the ventilator for most of the morning but he was just not strong enough. I am very sorry."

The color drained from the young woman's face and tears filled her eyes. She began to shake, and the nurse expelled the contents of the syringe into the IV line currently attached to her arm. She quickly collapsed onto the pillow. The nurse knew fully well that sedating the poor woman would do nothing; like putting a Band-Aid on a broken leg. She would eventually wake up, then again have to relive the terrible torture. But she did as she was told.

Bethany laid on the pillow, her body unmoving. Her eyes continued to bleed tears, even as she laid there, unconscious.

I was being watched

Time and space seem to move around me at an alarming pace and I had the strangest feeling that I was being watched. Not from the shadows, I had had enough of that feeling already, thank you. At first, the sensation was that of being on television or in a movie, but no, that's not accurate either. It was as if I was being cared for. Like so many doctors and nurses running around, tending to machines that prolonged life. More often than not, it was a life not worth prolonging. From the outside, one might think that I was clearly insane. I had finally gone mad. All those years that I had shunned the mental health industry and ridiculed it as nothing more than pure nonsense, and here I was an arm's length away from a straitjacket and a padded cell.

From the other side of my vision, a piercing green light blinded me and I was instantly brought back to reality. Or at least a reality that I was familiar with. I was on the Interstate. If I had to guess, I would say that it was close to 9:00 AM, though guessing the exact time was never one of my talents. The drive back into the city cleared my head of the horrific calamity that happened back in Middleton. And yet I was still as confused as ever. Even now, as I write these words, the events of that previous evening are fleeting. I'm still unsure as to why I was there in the first place. There's so much fog, not only in my mind but my heart as well. What have I become? Where am I headed? It's the same old cliché story; it seemed like only yesterday that I was happy. I had a wonderful apartment on the upper west side, where all the cool kids live. I was adored by my friends and envied by some that weren't. My career was finally headed in the right direction. So, where had I gone wrong? What decision did I make that set me on this path? My mind was a torrent of incoming questions, questions that I had no answer for.

I turned onto Meacham and drove north. My belly craved attention and nothing would soothe my soul more successfully than a plateful of fried doughnuts from Carol's Diner. So many nights alone, after work, I would need a plate. Not want, like someone may want a new car or the want of the opposite sex, but need; a need so glaringly defined, as when a body lusts for heroin. They're that good. The taste of sugar and cinnamon drizzled with warm chocolate appeared like acid on my tongue and I began to feel stronger – like my old self again. So much so that a smile graced the once wounded corners of my tender face, and suddenly the world was right once again. I pulled out my cell and dialed. The voicemail engaged.

You've reached James Burkhouse. I'm sorry but I am unavailable at this time. Please leave a message and I will return your call as soon as I can. Thank you.

James and I had been closer than Twix for most of our college days. Three years ago, he accepted an offer from my firm, and I've been his boss ever since. An annoyingly single brute with a bodybuilder's physique but the appetite of a hippo. We had actually met in middle school. We were both Sixth graders trying desperately not to get beaten up by the much larger and less educated Eighth graders. It was a challenge that I was able to easily avoid. James, however, stood his ground at every chance he got. Oftentimes I would swear to you that he went asking for trouble. What always astonished me, and the rest of our small group of friends, is that no matter how terrible the trouble was, James always came out of it unscathed. More times than not it was the opponent that would require some tending to. Out of all of us, James was the one that we knew would always be able to take care of himself.

"It's Sunday," I said out loud. "Where could he possibly be?"

With my phone in my hand, I made it back up the stairs to my apartment and quickly pressed the button to hear my messages; of which there were twenty seven. The first of which being from the one and only Joseph Bricker: my boss. He sounded quite upset. A client of mine had contacted him – displeased with my absence. Interesting. The next seven messages were similar. Baffled: I rang Joseph in an attempt at explaining my delinquency. Though I had no clear idea what was going on. It was Sunday. As of the previous Friday, I knew nothing of a client that required my attention.

"Walter!" Oh boy. "You useless motherfucker! Where the hell have you been? I have been trying to get a hold of you for over a week."

"Over a week? Joseph, that's impossible. It's Sunday. I was just in the office on Friday evening."

"You were supposed to meet with Richard Hassman Monday

afternoon. He called me on Tuesday screaming that you never showed up. Now he's taking his twelve and a half million dollars to another firm, you jerk."

There was a brief silence on the other line which allowed me to feel stunned. How had I lost a week?

"I want you in the office right now. Do you understand me?"

"Yes."

"Do you understand me?"

"Yes, sir," I answered again.

"You either answer me now or don't bother coming in!" There was an intense, low-frequency growl on the other end and I stiffened in fear. I told him that I had answered and that I would be there in fifteen minutes.

"I guarantee that if you're not here in fourteen minutes, I will drive to your slum of an apartment, take a carving knife and drive it right into your skull, you miserable cocksucker. After I'm done with you, I will mail your skin to your mother in Hell."

There was a fiendish laugh, another growl, and I could swear that I heard a woman crying in the background: my Penelope. Knowing that Bricker was not married or even had a girlfriend, I had the sense that something fiendish was afoot. I hung up the phone and sat down exhausted on the couch. Had I really lost a week? I felt a bead of sweat drip down my forehead and I brought my hand up to wipe my head. It wasn't sweat. It was blood from the knife protruding from my head. I smiled. The knife felt real enough but this had to be another dream. A knock came to the door and I got up. Nobody. I shut the door and walked towards the bathroom.

Knock knock.

I turned towards the door, astonished that I was still somewhere sleeping; deep inside a seemingly terrible dream. But I was not going to be fooled this time. No fake knife was going to scare me; no bloody box lying in wait.

Knock knock.

"Go away!"

"Walter! It's James! Let me in!"

"James?" I called – running back to the door and disengaging the deadbolt. Like a man on fire, he burst through the door. "What the hell?”

Bethany watched, and waited.

1971

Bethany watched from behind the wheel of a broken-down Ford Mustang, a burning cigarette between her fingers. She sat and smiled as folks dressed in suits, tuxedos, and expensive gowns entered the country club. The Mustang sat back behind the cars of employees.

She watched as car after car stopped and dropped off passengers while two young valets parked their vehicles. She was watching and waiting; waiting for one car in particular. She took a drag from the cigarette and thumbed the revolver in her lap. She learned of the event while reading the announcement in the local newspaper and quickly drove down state so as not to miss it.

Smoke billowed from the open window. The humidity was stifling but still, she waited. She would wait forever if she had to. She was determined as ever to see this through. She had purchased the gun a week before from a pawn shop that specializes in no-questions-asked transactions. The gun was loaded. She waited. Another car crested the hill to the entrance of the club. The valet ran to the driver's side and the couple exited the car. Thirty seconds later, another car approached and she lit another cigarette and remained calm. The sun fell below the trees and released its grip of breathtaking heat.

After another five minutes, a line of three cars approached the entrance, each one a long, black Cadillac. She waited and watched closely. The doors of the third and final car opened and a woman in a beautiful white wedding gown stepped out. The groom took her by the hand and Bethany exited the Mustang, the gun gripped tightly in her right hand. She walked briskly between the many cars already parked there and strolled up to the steps leading to the entrance. The bride and groom, along with a group of friends, were waiting there by the door. Bethany approached.

"Beatrice!" she called. Beatrice turned, her hands holding a bouquet of yellow and purple flowers. Standing not fifteen feet from her was her sister Bethany. Having not seen her sister for some time, Beatrice was shocked. She was even more shocked when Bethany raised her hand to reveal the handgun she held. "Don't move."

"Beth, what are you doing?" But Bethany didn't answer. She continued to stand still in front of the building holding her sister at bay. Those with Beatrice, including her new husband, shouted in fear. Bethany's grip on the gun tightened. She felt the trigger move. She saw that Beatrice was speaking; yelling at her – her face full of tears. But the only sound that she heard was that of the gun's hammer hitting the bullet in the chamber.

The shot went wide and Bethany struggled to pull the hammer back once again, stepping closer to the newlyweds. The rest had scattered after the initial shot, running inside the building. Before she had time to pull the trigger again, the glass door opened and a tall man with graying black hair stepped out.

"Bethany! What in the hell are you doing?" Bethany stared in disbelief at the sight of her father. The gun in her hand shook as her focus switched from her sister to her father. Why did he have to come out here? It was there that the goals for the evening had changed and Bethany pointed the gun at her father. Sirens could be heard in the distance and she brushed them away like a bug in her ear. Her father stepped closer.

"Bethany, please put down the gun." Another explosion and

then the man fell to the ground, a crimson rosette blossomed on his shoulder. Bethany stepped forward, pointing the gun directly at his head. A barrage of raised voices erupted behind her and suddenly she was face down on the concrete. Her arms felt as though they were going to snap off. A man with a deep voice was speaking to her but she could make nothing of it. Before she knew it, she was lifted off the ground and lead to a car, a police car, where she sat for near an hour in quiet contemplation.

Beatrice knelt over her father, blood staining the purity of her dress. She held his hand as paramedics worked on keeping him stable for the ride to the hospital. The bullet had gone straight through his body, shattering his collarbone in the process. He was in a great deal of pain. He would require months of physical therapy but thankfully, he would live. The wound was not life-threatening. Luckily for everyone there, Bethany was a bad shot.

Back in the police car, Bethany watched out the window as life passed by. Tears raced down her cheek. Not because she had been arrested but because she had missed: twice. The fierce heat of the summer evening could be felt through the window. The officer with the deep voice spoke from in front of her.

"What happened back there?" She remained silent, watching the world pass by in a torrent of red, yellow, and green lights.

At the police station, she was booked and fingerprinted, then placed in a holding cell with four other women of varying age and criminal charges – one of them being extremely pregnant. Bethany stood at the cell door, looking fervently out of the five-inch square Plexiglass window.

"Have a seat, darlin'," an older lady told her; seated in the corner, scratching at a blister on the top of her hand. "We're all gonna be here for a while."

For the first time in her life, Bethany was afraid. She knotted her fingers and hung her head in defeat as she took a seat on the hard wooden bench.

"What's your name, darlin'?" the older lady asked.

"Beth."

"What are you in here for?" the pregnant lady asked. Bethany didn't answer. She just sat with her knees up and her chin to her chest. "Don't be upset, honey. We're all here for something. My name is Catelyn. I got hit for selling cocaine to an undercover cop.

Sylvia over there, she's a transfer from Kansas City. She was arrested last year for stabbing her husband: twenty-two times."

Sylvia stood and walked over to sit next to Bethany. "I got tired of the constant abuse, so I put the mother fucker out of his misery."

Bethany looked up at Sylvia and smiled. Catelyn continued. "This here is Greta. We don't know her actual name because she doesn't speak so we just call her Greta. And last but not least…" Catelyn pointed to the tall black girl sitting on the floor, shuffling through a deck of cards. "This is Angel. She robbed a gas station and accidentally killed the poor sap behind the counter."

"I wasn't gonna kill him, bitch. He pulled out a gun first. It was self-defense."

"Right. So," Catelyn turned to Bethany. "What are you here for?"

Bethany raised her head and thought about the question. She was ashamed of being there. She didn't belong in jail. She was not one of them, and she felt out of sorts. She wiped her face and stood.

"Attempting to ruin my sister's life," she told them.

Sylvia turned to her. “Well, darlin’, that doesn’t sound like much of a crime.” They laughed.

“My crime was that I have yet to be successful.”

Take this to Walter

"Walter." He stood before me with his hands on his knees, a leather bag strapped to one shoulder, attempting to catch his breath. It was James. That was for certain. But he clearly wasn't himself. His long blonde hair was wet with sweat and his clothes were dirty and torn into rags. There were burn marks on his raw bloodied hands and he smelled of old dirt. "Jesus, Walter! Lock the door would you please?"

I did as he instructed and he then ran to the window and peered nervously outside.

"What's the matter, old friend?" He didn't answer. Instead, he ran room to room. Checking under the bed and looking in closets. He lifted the couch and checked underneath. "What are you doing, James?"

"Checking your apartment. Making sure we're alone."

"We're alone. I assure you."

After he had inspected the entire apartment – satisfied that we were, as I had said, alone – he tossed the bag on the floor and sat, with his face in his hands. I went to him, placing my hand on his shoulder. His hands shook noticeably, and I instantly forgot about Joseph and the knife and the growling baby.

"Talk to me."

"Yesterday, I went to Christy's. She had invited me over for dinner. I was apprehensive because I was planning on breaking it off with her. I accepted, thinking that if I were going to do it, I would be a man and not break up with her over the phone. Before I left my house though, I received a phone call." He hesitated here and I got the impression that he was holding something back or that there was a part of this narrative that he didn't want to share with me. I was inquisitive but tried to remain calm. Eventually, and with a number of deep breaths, he continued. "It was you. It was you, Walter – on the phone. You were raving about something with Debra. You said that you had killed her. You sounded mad. I didn't even know that you were seeing her again."

I didn't know how to respond. I wasn't seeing Debra again. As a matter of fact, I hadn't seen the girl in over five years. James stood and lumbered into the kitchen for a glass of water. He remained standing – uncomfortable like there was a weight on his shoulders that was getting more and more difficult to throw off.

"Killed Debra?" I asked, "What would make you think that I would do something like that?"

"You sounded sincere. You demanded that I drive all the way out to Middleton so that together we could bury the body. It was terrifying. And there was someone else there with you, a man by the sound of it, but much older. He was screaming but I couldn't tell what he was saying. What is going on, Walter?"

"Nothing's going on. I did not kill Debra. I spent all day and night with Penelope. We went shopping in the city then had a delightful dinner at Randolph's."

"Penelope? Who's Penelope?"

I stammered. "You remember Penelope," I told him. "She's..." Wait, I tried to recall the night that I had introduced them to each other but couldn't. There was no Penelope, was there? She was a figment; a fracture upon my cortex, a needle prick on the tip of my finger. The taste of bile rose to my tongue and I faltered slightly.

Penelope? “Never mind.”

I joined James in the kitchen and poured us both a tumbler of scotch.

“That’s not all,” he said as a matter of fact. “After the call with you ended, I gathered my things and was ready to set out to Middleton when a knock came to the front door. I wasn’t expecting company so you can understand my bewilderment at seeing an older, well-dressed gentleman standing in the hallway. He wore a finely tailored black suit and oddly styled hat. The grin he held on his wrinkled face was off-putting. Showing far too much rotted teeth. I asked him his business but he did not answer. I got the impression that he was unable to speak. I asked again and he held out his hands. He was holding a box. It was quite lovely actually, very ornate – red, with brass fittings. He held it out to me as if I were to take it from him. I did so and he left instantly.”

“The box!” I said out loud but more to myself. I felt dizzy. I knew of this box that James spoke of. I had seen it before. Hadn’t I? Though I was clearly feeling apprehensive, James appeared to relax somewhat and we both moved to the living room and sat across from each other.

“I didn’t want to open it, you see. You have to believe me when I say that I was compelled by something or someone. I set it on the coffee table and lifted the hatch, which I might add was quite extraordinary. It was the shape of some wild animal. Handcrafted I’m sure.”

James reached for the leather bag and opened its flaps. He glanced inside and was reluctant but eventually pulled out the box and placed it on his lap.

“Resting inside the box was this note.”

From his front pocket, James produced a torn piece of paper. But it wasn’t so much paper as it was – I can’t believe I’m even attempting to say this – skin. It was neatly folded twice and he handed it to me. I didn’t open it right off. I simply held it – feeling its weight. It felt and looked old, and, dare I say, alive. Warily, I unfolded it. My heart raced in my chest and I could feel my pulse through my clothes. The dizziness increased to a feeling of pure nausea.

Written on the vellum in dark red ink was an obvious message to me.

Take this to Walter.

I looked again at the box. Why was it to have come to me? The boar's head clasp stared at me as I lifted it from its place and opened the lid. Seeing nothing of interest, I rested the lid back down. Upon doing so, the world around me changed; shifted even. It felt as if I were trapped inside a cerebral cyclone of memories and thoughts. I was able to focus on everything yet nothing at all. I had to see it all at once or nothing. I chose nothing and closed my eyes, waiting for the event to cease. Why in God's name could I not have a normal life? Nothing is real anymore. I want what's real. **I WANT WHAT'S REAL!!!**

Marty, I think my water broke!

1973

Beatrice held her swollen belly with love, her Mother's afghan draped over her lap. She wanted to read but she felt that her mind might not be up for it. Pregnancy was nothing like what she expected. It was worse, so much worse. According to her doctor, the baby could come at any time now, she just needed to rest and wait. Her husband, Marty, was in the kitchen creating one of his world famous chicken, mustard, and pickle sandwiches - not for Beatrice, she was almost never hungry. He was slicing the sandwich in half at the corners when he heard the doorbell ring.

"I'll get it, honey," he called out from the kitchen.

Marty opened the door and a blast of hot air blew inside like an unwanted guest. He stepped outside and scratched his head of shiny brown hair; nobody was there. He stepped a little further down the front walk and lit a cigarette from his front pocket. He had never smoked in the house before, but now that Bea was pregnant, he didn't want her to smell it at all.

Stepping over the broken concrete on the sidewalk, he opened the garage door and pulled up a chair to finish the smoke. It was relaxing, and certainly fleeting. With a baby on the way, his time alone would be nonexistent. He took in a breath of self-polluted air and smashed out the butt in the ashtray. It was warm, almost too warm for September. Fall would arrive soon, then the evil snap of winter. Marty hated winter with a passion. He had tried many times to convince Beatrice to move south but she insisted that she wanted the baby born in her hometown. Reluctantly, he agreed but with the promise that they would move before the baby started school.

Beatrice stood – holding her inflated belly. She waddled carefully to the bathroom, hoping that this was it, it was time to have the baby. The bags were packed. They had been packed for weeks actually. Marty insisted on it.

She made it to the bathroom and sat. She had thought that it would be much easier to bring a blanket and pillow with her to cut down on travel time.

Back in bed, Marty rolled over and draped his arm across his wife's breasts. It comforted him to know that she was there and alright. Bethany smiled and caressed Marty's arm. Lovingly, she kissed his fingers then reached behind to grab his crotch. Marty instantly moaned and hardened with excitement. It had been several months since Beatrice had touched him in that way. Certainly, they couldn't go any further but he wasn't about to complain.

Bethany turned over in the darkened room and placed her mouth between his legs. Marty smiled with surprised pleasure. Beatrice must be in a wild mood because oral sex was not one of her favorite things. Perhaps it was due to all the swirling hormones. Yet, again, who was he to complain. He arched his back and felt all of the blood rush to his head as he finished. The intensity of the act took his breath away. At that moment the bedroom light clicked on.

"Marty, I think my water broke!" Marty looked down frantically at the woman whose head was still in his lap, then looked up to see his wife – her face red with rage. Marty held Bethany by the head but she was able to wiggle free and land a right hook square on his jaw.

Beatrice was unable to speak. Her contractions were coming closer and harder as she sat on the edge of the bed holding her belly

– tears of rage and disgust raked her face and stained her cheeks. Marty was still stunned on the bed and Bethany stood, wiping her mouth. Beatrice picked up a hand mirror and threw it at Bethany, missing her completely.

"Why?" It was the only word that she could say.

"Why?" Bethany answered, standing now at the bedroom door, a single drop of semen resting on her bottom lip. "Why? I'll tell you why, you little spoiled bitch!" Bethany seemed to gather her composure. For a moment she appeared to feel remorseful. It must have been an accident because no sooner had it started than it was gone and Bethany seemed to grow in size. "Precious little Bea. Mama's favorite. You really don't remember, do you? Remember when I told you what Daddy was doing to me? Remember when I told you that it was a secret? Well, guess what? The whole school found out, didn't they? Principal Logaman called me into the office, remember? There was Mom and Dad, sitting there looking embarrassed. They made me admit that I had made it all up – that it was all in my head. But it wasn't in my head, was it, Bea? You know it wasn't because you saw it, didn't you? You saw our own father rape me and you said nothing! You were there when I told Mom that

I wasn't making it up. You could've said something then but you didn't, did you? You could've done something to stop it all but you didn't, did you?"

Beatrice sat on the bed and cried – continuing to hold her belly.

"I'm sorry, Beth. I'm so sorry."

"Don't waste your tears on me, little sister. I'm better than you now. I've learned that everything I've ever wanted is right here. Trust me, Bea, what's yours will be mine."

Bethany exited the room and lifted the kitchen phone from its cradle. She picked up the shotgun that Marty left leaning against an antique desk, as the operator clicked on.

"Could you send an ambulance to 4237 Berkshire? My sister is in labor."

And just like the warm summer wind, Bethany was gone.

Your Father is Gone

I WANT WHAT'S REAL!

I must've said this out loud because instantly the convulsion radiating from my spinal column stopped and I was happy to open my eyes. As I did, I could sense that my wish for reality had not been granted. I was in a room of some kind. There were certainly windows because someone had left the blinds open and the sun was burning everything in white. It was so bright that I had to shield my eyes. They watered and I wiped them, trying desperately to focus in a vain attempt to escape from wherever I was. The smell of lilac hit my nose and I heard the faint melody of Vivaldi's 'Four Seasons'. I suddenly realized where I was and moved towards where I remembered the door to be. The light was intense and blinding. If I looked down through my fingers, I caught a glimpse of carpeting.

I stepped lively around a plastic table with a tea set, laid out with care. There were dolls everywhere. Many of them were in different stages of play. The carpeting was white, though I remember it to be an awful shade of blue.

I made it to the door and placed my hand on the knob and turned. The door opened without hesitation and I exited my sister Jillian's childhood bedroom. Once in the hallway, I took the stairs two at a time and set off towards the kitchen where I heard my mother's voice just now calling for me. The lilac smell was much stronger out here. So was the smell of bacon, and pancakes with maple syrup. Eggs for Dad, nobody else wanted any. Orange juice in a pitcher placed on the table. I sat and my mother smiled. Jillian, three years older than I, believed she was too cool for breakfast and sat on the stairs, talking to someone on the telephone. Mom filled my plate with all the things I loved, and I ate like it was to be my last. Dad sat there with his coffee, reading the paper while Mom kept shoveling food onto his plate. Dad never liked Mom's cooking, and he would tell her as much. I never understood it. I thought her food was delicious, but Dad would always say that she was trying to poison him. "If I wanted you dead, you'd be dead," she'd always tell him. And then without any hesitation, Dad would step away from the table, kiss Mom on the cheek and leave. Then it was just me and

Mom, alone at the table. It was summer so there was no school. Oftentimes I would find myself staying inside all day helping Mom with the dishes or whatever else she needed to be done around the house. Then there were other times that she would demand that I go outside and play, insisting that I stay away all day. Don't come in until I call you.

"Where have you been, Walter? I called you inside over an hour ago."

"I'm sorry, Mom. I guess I just didn't hear you."

"Oh, that's alright, darling."

She would be sitting in the living room watching the 'Wheel of Fortune' while working on some impossible puzzle. A glass of brown liquid always present. She was always working on a puzzle, and she never finished one of them. Not one.

The odd but pleasant smell of lilacs hit my nose again and I looked around the room. Dad was usually sitting there with her. They watched the Wheel together ceremoniously. They hated each other's company but they never missed a single episode. Kind of puts my own life in perspective, don't ya think?

I looked up at the telephone hanging on its hook on the wall next to the refrigerator, alone and unused. This was also out of the ordinary. Mom could sense a question coming on and she took a sip of the liquid and pulled a few loose strands of hair behind her ears.

"Your father is gone." She spoke gruffly. "Jillian too."

"Where did they go?" *And why wouldn't they take me?*

In place of an answer, she smiled at me and gently stepped away from the puzzle, picking up her glass in the process.

"I bet you're hungry, aren't you? My dear sweet boy." I smiled at the notion of more food and she was gone in a flash. "Look, Walter, I've made a pot roast for you. Just the way you like it, with carrots and roasted potatoes."

Truth be told, I never like pot roast no matter who was cooking it. But I could never say that to her. She sat at the table watching me eat. I really hated whenever she did that. And as soon as I had cleared my plate, she would fill it again and smile. She seemed so happy. How could I disappoint her by saying that this was the worst thing I had ever put in my mouth? And just to be clear, I could rummage through the neighbor's garbage cans and find a number of things that were far more edible than what I had been forced to eat. Eventually, I would tell her that I was stuffed. It's delicious Mom but I can't eat another bite. That sort of thing.

"Walter?"

I looked up from the table to find my mother at the foot of the stairs. She was wearing pajamas and slippers, and her hair was in tight curlers. Sometimes my mom would drink. Jillian told me once that she remembered a time when Mom never drank. Sometimes my mom would drink a lot. Sometimes my mom would drink so much that I wished she would just pass out. Apparently, that was not going to be this night.

"Yes, Mom, I'll do the dishes," I answered. "You go ahead and lie down. I'll clean up."

"Walter," she said again, almost whispering. "I want to show you something first."

She turned slowly and walked up the stairs. I ran after her, thinking that in her state she just might take a fall and then I would have to explain that to my Dad, who did not drink but would not understand.

She reached the top of the stairs and stood there waiting for me. The look on her face was chilling but it was likely due to the low wattage lighting in the hallway. Still, she moved slower than usual, not talking but stepping somberly down the hall. We passed my bedroom first and I thought for a quick minute that she was going to go into Jillian's room and ask why I had been in there, but she walked by the room, heading in the direction of her and Dad's room.

I could see, even in the poor lighting, that the door was closed. This was another oddity. Unless he was sleeping, Dad always insisted on leaving the door open. He claimed that it assisted with the home's air circulation. Is that true?

Mom wrapped her fingers around the doorknob and stopped. She took a sip of the liquid then pushed the door open. Once again, I was greeted by an intensely bright light. I brought my hands up to cover my eyes and my Mother guided me over to the side of the bed. My feet suddenly felt wet and I had the sensation that I falling down. Why was I always falling? At last, my eyes became accustomed to the light and I brought my hands down to my sides. My eyes focused on my mother's king-sized bed that Dad had bought her a number of years ago. Dad was laying on his back with his arms out like a bird's wings. I didn't understand what she was showing me until I was able to focus more and I saw that Jillian was there, lying next to him. Her arms were across her chest, and there was a strange look on her face, like she was surprised. Dad had a different look. He looked pissed. I looked back at Mom who was sitting at her vanity brushing her hair and looking at me through the mirror. Her eyes betrayed nothing and I turned back to the bed.

Dad had a hole in his chest the size of a basketball. I gasped, warm tears fell from my eyes, though I would not cry. His head was resting peacefully on his pillow, though by the look of the wound at his neck it was not attached to his body. Rich red blood pooled onto the carpeting and turned my feet a sickening brown.

Jillian had cuts to her face that almost looked like someone had tried drawing on her with a knife. The hole in her stomach was not so much a hole as it was a bowl of blood and gore. Both of her legs were missing and I wanted to find them and reattach them. Resting on the bed with them were about a hundred or so sprigs of lilac. I felt a rage inside me that I had never felt before. The tears were streaming down my face in a rainstorm and I looked to my mother. She just smiled.

"Time for bed, darling." And she calmly shooed me out of her room and slammed the door. In a panic, I ran downstairs and out of the house to the Forbert's next door. When I reached the front door, the porch light went out like a match in a desert wind. It was the same down the entire block. No one would help. I ran back to the house, frightened out of my wits. I picked up the phone and dialed the police. I was sitting outside crying like a baby when two squad cars stopped in front of the house. One sat with me, asking questions while the other three searched the house. I explained to them that they wouldn't need their guns. My mother would go peacefully, even quietly. But when the screech from the officer's hand-held reached my ears, I knew it had become worse than I could ever possibly imagine.

No one would help

The room was bright again and I knelt down and felt the soft carpeting with my hands. The wretch of an anguished sob bellowed from my soul as I saw my sister's empty room again. Her bed made neatly. Her dresses hung in the closet, arranged by color and popularity. The tea set remained untouched for years. Even as she got older, she wouldn't take it down, nor would she play with it. I sat down on her bed and wiped away the tears. On her walls were pictures of friends and posters of different bands. The Ramone's, The Clash, and her favorite: Green Day. Though I would never tell her so, not to her face anyway, I always thought that Jillian was cool. She had a crazy punk rock style that I was never able to achieve.

I sat up and felt something shift underneath the blanket. Curious, I reached under and pulled it out. It was a notebook. Better yet, it was a diary. She was always writing. Let me take that back. She was always on the phone. If she wasn't on the phone, she could be found in her room with her stereo on writing in a book; this book. I held the thing in my hands, succumbing to the knowledge that she was the last person to touch this – any of this. My heart bled in agony. I missed her. I hated her guts, but I missed her.

The cover was, like any other teenage girls' spiral notebook, adorned with scribbles and doodads that made sense only to her. Do I dare? Would she forgive me? Would I forgive me? Certainly not. I would never forgive her if she went traipsing through my belongings. So, I placed it back on the bed and stood. Was this part of the dream? It had to be. This room no longer held any reality for me. In truth, it didn't even exist anymore. None of this did. That's the point though, isn't it? What the hell was all this for?

I plucked a tiny teacup from the table and held it. I don't know why. Not even now do I understand why but I dropped it in my pocket and sat back down on the bed. Forgive me, Jilli.

Nervously, I opened the notebook to the first page. I felt a sudden stream of guilt but pressed on. Her handwriting was perfectly styled, flourished with loops and curls. I read with a well of tears, unable to properly focus.

I hate school. Randy told John that I liked him today. I don't like him. I never liked him, but Cindy told Randy that I did. I hate school. Troy Rutledge was looking at me in English class yesterday. He can look at me any day.

I caught Walter picking his nose yesterday morning. Let's skip a few pages. Shall we?

I heard Mom talking to herself today. It was funny at first but then she started yelling and screaming, sometimes in different languages. I was frightened. I remember a time when Mom was kind and loving. She's different now. I went to her room and tried to comfort her but she slammed the door in my face. She's getting worse. And now that she's drinking more, it's like I don't have a mother. Ever since Uncle Mark died, she's never been the same.

I skipped a few more pages concerning high school and boys and smoking pot. Boy, I really wish I had known that last one.

She came into my room late one night last week while I was sleeping and pulled me out of bed. I told her to stop but I don't think she could hear me. She held my hand so tight that I couldn't let go so I just walked with her, hoping that at some point she would let go. She pulled me up to the attic. I had never been up there. Walter goes up there all the time with his stupid friends.

She made me sit on the dirty floor while she sifted through some boxes. I tried to scoot away but I could tell that she was watching me, holding me at bay. She made a strange sound like a baby crying once she found what she was looking for and placed it on the attic floor in front of me. It was a box. Like a jewelry box, I think. But it was old and dusty. Not like any jewelry box that I would ever have. It was wooden and painted red and on the clasp was an ugly animal's head. She motioned for me to open it. As I did, the lid made a sound like a creaking door moving on rusty hinges. Inside was a dirty old brass key. She told me to take it and not tell anyone, so I did. Then she passed out on the attic floor and I went back down to bed. I still have the key. I just don't understand why she told me to take it. The more I think about it – I don't think that was my mom. She didn't feel alive. It was like she was a ghost.

And yet another few pages.

Dad told me last night that we're moving. No, wait. He didn't use the word moving. He said we were leaving. I asked him why and he said 'to take your mother somewhere where she will get the help that she needs'.

I'm officially afraid of her now. I'm afraid to go home after school; afraid to go to bed; afraid to get out of bed. Mom doesn't know yet that Dad is taking her away. I will miss her – the way she used to be before... Before the darkness took her.

I should've aimed for his head

1977

Throughout the history of the latter part of the twentieth century, no sound produced more jubilation from a child than that of the annoying recorded bells and whistles of the neighborhood ice cream man. Like the Pied Piper of Hamelin leading the rats out of the city, the ice cream man led children on an adventure. An adventure of over-priced madness. A sugar coma inducing free-for-all, set to the tune of 'The Wheels on the Bus Go Round and Round'.

Little Jillian almost fell running out the door to join the rest of the neighborhood gang in purchasing their favorite summertime treat. Jillian's favorite was chocolate and vanilla on a stick in the shape of Mickey Mouse – including gumballs for eyes.

Jillian ran, looking behind her every few seconds to make sure her mother was with her to carry the money. At four years old, Jillian was a handful.

"Hurry up, Mama!" Jillian screeched.

"He's not going anywhere, Jilli," Beatrice told her.

They reached the truck with a group of kids and parents. One mother saw Beatrice and rushed over. Beatrice cringed inwardly at the sight of Mary Peterson. Mary was nice enough and she always meant well, but if asked, Beatrice would say that Mary could be a little annoying; not unlike the never-ending drone of music, still being played from the ice cream truck's loudspeaker.

"Well hey there, Bea! How you doin', girl?" Beatrice gave her a friendly hug as the neighborhood children screamed and begged for ice cream.

"Hangin' in there I suppose." Beatrice laughed at herself. Mary was from somewhere down south. Deep south like Georgia or South Carolina. Her accent was pure Southern Belle and Beatrice often caught herself making fun of it. If Mary had been offended by it, she had never said so. Mary placed her hand on Beatrice's swollen belly.

"Do you know yet?" she asked.

"It's a boy, Mary." Beatrice smiled and squeezed her hand.

Jillian came running, holding out her ice cream for her mother to open. Girls in pink shorts and pig tails waited for her.

"Mama, who's that?" Jillian pointed at the front door of their house and the woman standing there. The woman looked a little like her mother but with shorter hair. Beatrice stiffened at the sight of her sister Bethany. She stood on the front stoop as if waiting there for someone or something. Beatrice took Jillian by the hand and marched up the sidewalk towards the house. If Beatrice was afraid, she refused to show it. She would no longer allow Bethany to ruin her life. Whatever had happened in the past was in the past, she would not be afraid of her anymore.

Beatrice stopped at the front walk and pushed little Jillian behind her, to shield her from the evil that was her sister Bethany.

"What are you doing here, Beth?" Beatrice snarled and Bethany stammered, not entirely certain what to say. It was a logical question. Why had she come? Why had she chosen this day to show up at her sister's house? Was there a reason – an agenda? To Beatrice, Bethany was nobody. She had stopped caring, stopped hurting, and stopped worrying about her. No matter how mean she was, Beatrice always thought that one day Bethany would come around. Even after she had threatened to shoot her, she still loved her. All that changed when she found her in bed with her husband. It wasn't Marty's fault, of course. Bethany knew what she was doing. That night, the night that Jillian came into the world, was the night she decided that she would no longer be afraid of her sister.

"Do you want to leave on your own or shall I call the police to remove you?"

"Bea… I don't want to fight with you." Beatrice looked at her sister. She had been crying. From the look on her face, she had been crying for a long time. "I don't want to fight with anyone anymore."

Beth sat down on the steps as the neighborhood girls came to usher Jillian away. Her red face fell into her hands and she began to sob. Beatrice fought back the urge to go to her. She remained strong. Bethany had her chance.

"Jillian's getting so big."

"How dare you say her name." Beatrice fumed and stepped closer to her home. "Don't you ever say her name again."

"But, Bea, she's my niece."

“No, she’s not! Jillian knows nothing about you! And as far as I’m concerned, that’s how it’s going to stay.” She held her pregnant belly. “And my son will never know you either.”

“Son?” Bethany stood and righted herself. “You’re having a boy?”

Bethany stepped off the stoop and walked towards her sister at the front of the house. The closer Bethany got, the more she appeared broken. Beatrice knew that she had been taking drugs but she didn’t know what. Her hair was matted and what was left of her make-up was smeared. A slightly faded bruise around her right eye topped off the look. She stopped just two feet from her sister. Beatrice refused to move. Both sisters were deadlocked; neither wanting to move but praying that the other would. After a short while, Beatrice saw fresh tears drop down Bethany’s cheeks, and for the first time in years, Beatrice let herself go.

“I’m sorry, Bea.” Bethany moved in to embrace her sister but Beatrice moved back.

“Don’t.”

“I want my sister back. I want my family back.”

Beatrice threw her hands in the air. “You want your sister back? You never had a sister! I don’t even remember a time when you were nice to me.”

“Beatrice, please.”

“Have you been out to see Mom and Dad?” Quickly Bethany changed. Her attitude was that of the old Bethany. The thought of her father brought back the old feelings of anger and hatred.

“You know what he did to me, right?” she asked with a grimace. “How could I ever go back there?”

Bethany swayed and fell to the sidewalk, her hands held her upright and Beatrice sat down to meet her gaze. She took her hand and Bethany smiled. Not her usual evil grin but an actual smile. The smile of knowing you are loved.

“Bethany, I want to believe you. God, I want to believe you. But how can I ever trust you again? How can I? After everything that’s happened?”

For several minutes the two sisters sat in silence, their hands gripping the other’s tightly. Suddenly, from behind Beatrice, Jillian came running over. She smiled at Bethany.

"Mama, can I play basketball at Bobby's house?"

"Yes, little one." Beatrice patted her daughter on the backside then stood, pulling her sister up with her.

"I love that she calls you Mama."

"It wasn't anything I did," Beatrice told her. "She just started calling me Mama."

"And now you have a son on the way."

"Yes, he'll be a Christmas baby."

"Bea, I want to know them, and I want them to know me."

Beatrice took in a deep breath. She loved summertime. She remembered a time when her and Bethany got along; actually loved each other. She felt a pang of guilt for allowing it to get so bad for so many years.

"I'm sorry, Beth." Beatrice looked down at her bare feet, ashamed. "I should've helped you. I should've stood up for you. It's no wonder you acted the way you did."

Like so many other women, Bethany reached out and touched her sister's belly. "I had a son," Bethany admitted.

Beatrice looked up, surprised. “Where is he now?”

“It was a difficult delivery. Fourteen hours because something about me not being dilated enough.” She took a breath. “After he was born, he went into respiratory distress, and his heart wasn’t functioning properly. They put him on a little baby ventilator, but there had already been too much damage. He died the next day.”

“I’m sorry, Beth.” Bethany smiled back at her sister. Beatrice held in a question. It was an obvious question. The same question that anyone would ask. She needed to ask but felt horrible for doing it. It was truly none of her business. “Who’s the father?”

It was the question that Bethany knew was coming. The same question that her therapist asked her in jail, and the counselors at the Brady House. It was a fair question, and one that she was finally willing to answer. She sighed and let her head fall to her chest. For Beatrice, she didn’t have to answer. She knew.

“No!” It was a shocking revelation. “Does he know?”

“No. I tried telling him once. When they came to visit me in jail. After I put a bullet in his shoulder. I should’ve aimed for his head.” She looked up at her sister and they both let out a laugh.

“I have to go.” Bethany told her.

“Where are you staying?”

“The Brady House. It’s a rehab-halfway house. I’m on furlough for the afternoon.” A sarcastic smirk appeared on Bethany’s face and they both found themselves laughing again. It felt good for the both of them to feel together. It might take a while but maybe this was a chance to become a family again.

“Let me give you a ride,” Beatrice offered.

“Not on your life, sis. I love this weather and I’m gonna use this time to fill my lungs with life. The life that I have been missing out on.”

The two embraced and Bethany set off on the mile and a half walk. Beatrice smiled at her good fortune. Could she trust her sister after all this time? She did not know, but she wanted to. She turned her face to the west and filled her eyes with the oncoming sunset. The fiery orange and red of the day’s end made her feel warm. Marty would be home from work soon and they would walk the neighborhood with Jillian. A tradition that she refused to sway from. Soon, another child would join in on that tradition.

Beatrice thought of a name for the boy. She looked down at her belly – getting bigger by the day, she thought. She thought of the man that she had as her father. She needed to come to grips with the truth and make him admit what he had done. But still, she always knew him as a kind and gentle man. He and Marty always got along well, like good friends. She smiled at the realization. She had her boy's name. She would name him after her own father: Walter.

I Love the Smell of Grass

She's still here. Why is she still here? She left yesterday. Dad took her away. I saw them leave with Walter. I didn't want to go with. I didn't even want to say goodbye. That's not my Mom. I said goodbye to my Mother long before. But she's here now. She's back. I can hear her downstairs talking with Walter. Dad should be down there as well, reading his paper and drinking that awful coffee. I will never understand how people can drink their coffee black. It's so bitter and gross.

I want Dad to take me away. Just me. Walter can stay here with her. I don't want to be here anymore with her.

I just got off the phone with Jody and she told me that she saw my Mom at the grocery store and that she was acting strangely. I didn't tell her any of what was happening. I'm far too embarrassed for that. Jody said that she went to say hello to Mom, and Mom stared at her like she was on drugs or something and that she started yelling at her. Worst of all, Jody backed away and watched my Mother throw all of her groceries on the floor, then stomp away.

Last page.

Why is she being so nice to me now? She seems like the Mother I know but I don't want to trust it. I don't want to believe it. She made breakfast this morning and was smiling and talking like she was back to her normal self. I actually saw her sitting in the family room attempting a puzzle. She used to love putting together puzzles. It was as if working through the pieces made her feel better. But I'm not buying it. I can't put my finger on it but something is off. I can't explain it other than to say that she is moving differently. It's almost like someone or maybe something is controlling her and forcing her to act normal.

I love my brother Walter. I really do. But if he doesn't take a fucking shower soon, I am seriously going to freak out.

I love the smell of grass. The scent of freshly cut grass is my favorite smell of summer. I take that back. It's my favorite smell of all time. I love sitting out on the front porch when dad is mowing the lawn and that smell just infects every pour of my body. They should make a perfume out of that. Or at least a candle. I always help Dad gather the mulch just so I can be around that smell. I love the smell of grass.

Then that was it. Her last statement in this book was to say that she loved the smell of grass. Poignant, don't you think? I set the book back into its hiding place and stood, once again looking about my sister's bedroom. She mentioned a key. A key to what, I wonder. I had intended on finding it, or at the very least, look for it. But as my vision became less and less blurry, I took notice that the situation was once again puzzling. Something was gravely different. The bright light from the window was still frying my corneas to the point of blindness but there were no longer any windows. The white light was coming from above. Was I dead? Was I being led into the light of the afterlife? If so, I did not wish to go.

There was a cacophony of sounds. The rush of air being pushed out; the metallic whir of a machine, doing whatever it does; the irritating pulse of something beeping – keeping all the other machines in precise time. There were curtains and a glass door on the other side of the curtains. People were everywhere, bumping into me without excusing themselves. It was quite rude actually. A tall man was bending over something large on the opposite side of the room. I couldn't catch a glimpse of it but it appeared to be of some grand interest.

Walter

That was not a hallucination. Someone clearly and without hesitation, spoke my name, and they said it on purpose as if to gain my attention.

Walter

Again. This time it seemed to be closer, or perhaps louder. I could not determine the difference.

"Walter, it's me. Jillian. Can you hear me?"

"Jillian?" I whispered. "Where are you? I can hear you but I can't see you."

Just then a figure moved towards me with a laboring gait. She was wearing a spring dress of yellow and purple flowers. Her hair was pulled back into a low ponytail: the way she always wore it. Around her neck was a leather rope choker with two polished metal rings. She had found them at the playground one afternoon and fashioned a necklace out of them. People would constantly ask her of their meaning but she told them that it was a secret that she would never tell. This was my sister Jillian. And now among the chaos of whatever this room was that I was standing in and whatever was going on inside of it, she stood before me smiling.

"But you're dead," I told her as if she hadn't known. Tearing up yet again. "You died years ago. I remember your funeral."

"Yes, I'm dead, Walter, and you need to wake up. Wake up, Walter."

"Wake up? I didn't realize that I was sleeping."

"You're not."

Her words stunned me like an electrical current and I stood frozen, remembering her how she once was. Even now she was my big sister. And as much as I loathe reminiscing about the good old days, it was difficult to not wax nostalgic.

"Remember Frankie Finch?"

"Yeah, why?"

"He's the Mayor now. Can you believe that? The same kid

that had the worst body odor ever, is now the Mayor."

"Walter. Dear brother. You need to wake up before it's too late."

"Before it's too late? Too late for what?"

She came closer like she wanted to whisper something to me. It was confusing. I saw her mouth move but her voice was lost. I explained to her that I couldn't hear her and she became sad. Not angry or upset but sad rather, like she was losing a contest or as if she were broken in some way and was unable to be repaired.

She could still hear me but her voice became nothing more than a reverberation. I caught hints of words and I realized that this hallucination might disappear as quickly as it appeared so I chose to not waste any more time. I needed her attention now.

"Jillian." She looked up into my eyes. "Where's the key?"

She shrugged her shoulders in an effort to communicate to me that she was unaware of what I was talking about.

"The key that Mother gave you in the attic." At once she became hideously angry, and I will not pretend that I don't know why. The only way I could possibly know about the key is if I had read her notebook. I don't blame her for being cross with me but I needed her to focus. "Jilli, listen to me, please. I'm sorry that I read it but I found it in your room and I missed you so. I thought it would help me to remember you."

She seemed to ease a bit at this and so I tried to ask her again but she put her finger to her lips in an attempt to silence me. She looked back at the scene in the room and stepped closer. She breathed another whisper in my ear and I swear to you that I believe I heard her. It was like a recording from years ago, with all the cracks and distortions. Yes, I heard her. I know where the key is. What I don't know is what the damn hell is it for. I nodded to let her know that I heard her and she smiled the prettiest smile. The smile that I remember. The smile of a little girl without a care in the world. That smile left her after Mom fell into the darkness.

"Walter. You must wake up now, please, Walter."

"Jillian, I'm here. I'm right here."

And just like that she faded into the chaos and could no longer hear me. Could anyone hear me?

"Hey! I'm right here!" I screamed to those in the room that were refusing to hear me. "HEY! CAN ANYBODY HEAR ME! STOP IGNORING ME! JILLIAN! JILLIAN!"

Marty Didn't Trust Her

1978

The morning of January twelfth began with a blizzard the likes that many had never seen before. More than two feet of snow fell in three hours time. The city was covered in a white blanket of cold powder. Luckily, Marty had made it home with his wife and their new baby boy. Walter arrived the afternoon before, weighing a full eight pounds and crowned in thick black hair, with a strawberry colored birthmark adorning his left eye. The nurses at the hospital announced that he was kissed by an angel.

The winter wind blew hard against the windows and doors, creating a draft of chilly air. Marty lit a fire in the fireplace while Beatrice sat covered and nursed her baby.

"I don't like it, Bea," Marty told his wife. "I don't trust her and I don't understand how you can."

At first Beatrice didn't react to his comment. It was clear that she didn't have an answer. How could she allow her sister in their home? Especially after all the trouble she had caused them. Less than a week ago, Bethany had visited and offered her assistance to her sister. A number of days Beatrice had been left at home alone while Marty went into work. Even if it was only for a few hours a day, Beatrice felt alone and vulnerable being so close to her delivery date. Beatrice asked her sister to stay and gave her the guest room. Now that the delivery was over, Marty had hoped that Bethany would leave.

"Martin, have you seen it outside lately?" Beatrice fumed. "We're are not sending my sister out in this. When the weather breaks we will send her home." Marty stomped into the kitchen. He understood that Beatrice was happy that she and her sister had repaired their relationship but the bitter truth was that Marty didn't trust her. He never would. And now he believed that his family was in jeopardy.

From the dining room, Bethany appeared, carrying an empty coffee cup and looking like she was recovering from a long night of drinking. Her hair had been cut short and she looked leaner, as if she had begun working out recently. Marty thought to himself that if he hadn't known better, he would've thought that she was his wife.

"Long night?" Marty asked sarcastically.

"Just a little cold," she answered while filling her cup. "I'll be fine."

Marty could detect the scent of bourbon and schnapps escaping from her pores like a vapor. Beatrice said that she was clean but clearly she wasn't. She was using them for a place to stay. Once she left the half-way house she had nowhere to go, and his poor wife fell for her shit. He watched her as she took her now steaming cup of coffee and trudged into the living room to sit next to her sister and the baby. He couldn't explain it, and he certainly wouldn't say a thing to his wife, not yet anyway, but there was something not quite right about this woman. Marty knew people. He was able to read them easily. That was his job. As a psychiatrist, he found that he could size people up fairly quickly and easily. Bethany had given him a run for his money. She wasn't as easy to read as the troubled couples and undisciplined children he spoke to every day, but he was certain that she wasn't here to be with her sister. She had an agenda. Beatrice spoke to him at length about her sister's past. She blamed her problems on their father, an abusive man that took advantage of her and cared nothing about it, even going as far as to produce a child with his own daughter. She tried to reassure him that Bethany's troubles were behind her, that she was no longer destructive. However, Marty wasn't so sure. She had already been there a week and showed no signs of leaving. She had no other place to go. Why would she leave? She would have no reason to go anywhere else.

"Martin!" Beatrice called from the living room.

He stepped in to see his wife standing next to the window – looking out onto the snowstorm. Bethany was holding his son. Jillian was seated next to her looking through a picture book. His daughter looked up at him wide-eyed and raced over to embrace his kneecaps. He smiled and sighed expressively. The anxiety washed away like waterfall and for a fleeting moment he thought that he had been overreacting. Beatrice carefully walked to him and took his hands in hers.

"Darling, I know that we had talked about putting off getting a nanny until I was ready to go back to work." Marty felt a surge of energy rise in him from somewhere near his gut. His blood sped through his veins. "Bethany has asked to take care of the kids while I go back to work." Beatrice paused here – giving her husband time to absorb the idea one sentence at a time.

"Bea – "

"I accepted."

"Darling," he pulled her into the kitchen. "I really don't think that's a good idea."

"Why not?"

"First of all, you just got out of the hospital. You are nowhere near ready to go back to work. And –"

"Marty," she cut him off. "I teach third graders. I will be just fine. I'm giving it two more weeks then I'm going back."

"What about Walter?"

"What about him? Bethany will be here with him and for Jillian when she gets off the bus."

Marty held his breath for a moment – calculating the possible responses to what he was going to say next. Neither of them had a positive outcome. He ran his fingers through his hair, an action of frustration that Beatrice knew all too well.

“That’s what I’m afraid of.”

“What’s that supposed to mean?”

“I don’t trust her. You know I don’t trust her. How can you leave her alone with our children? She tried killing you, remember? Then she broke into our house and sneaked into bed with me. Bea, I think it’s a bad idea. I know you think that she’s changed but I’m telling you: there’s something wrong about her, and putting her in charge of our children, well, I think she’s dangerous.”

Beatrice looked at her husband for a long moment. Seemingly longer than any other moment. She was angry but she chose not to show it. When they had a chance at privacy, she would take it up with him again. For now, she straightened and marched proudly back into the living room and sat next to Jillian on the couch. Marty watched her as she moved with such confidence. The image in front of him was one of happiness, and he gazed lovingly at his son, held in the arms of his sister-in-law. Bethany looked up and caught his eye. In that moment, Marty felt the hairs on the back of his neck stand at attention. Her eyes were that of pure evil, and Marty knew that from that moment on, he would do everything in his power to protect his family from her.

Why do I need to find the key?

I often have trouble sleeping. Not for the numerous reasons that you might think, but for the reasons that you might not think. I attempt to get comfortable. Though when I do it becomes either too warm or too cold. Perhaps, on those nights when the climate is just so and I believe that I might get a decent night's rest, I am struck by an intense feeling of anxiety; as if someone were continuously knocking on my head like it was a door. There are nights that I lay awake dreaming of cake, rich chocolate cake. I know it's ridiculous but of all the things that keep me awake, this would be the most benign. Cake I can deal with, strange folks trying to speak to me in my dreams is a bit more difficult. It's true, however. The moment my mind becomes at peace, I am spoken to. Let me try to explain. Have you ever had a dream that you thought was so real that you questioned whether it was actually a dream at all? Of course you have. When I dream, I am confronted by a group of people that I would swear are trying to speak to me from the other side. I say the other side because I have no other reasoning for it. Where else might they be talking to me from? Those persons that are speaking to me or at the very least trying to speak to me are of many sorts; young and old, man and woman. A young girl of roughly the age of six had approached me with a soccer ball one afternoon while I had collapsed on the couch in my office. She asked if I wanted to play. I told her that soccer wasn't really my sport but if she had a bat and a ball, I would give my best effort. The most recent conversation that comes to mind was with an older gentleman who appeared to be about 65, though he may have been much older. He wore faded jeans and a tan shirt under a corduroy jacket. His hair was shoulder length, not fully gray but on its way. He sat next to me at a café outside of Del Fromagio on a wonderfully warm evening. I wanted to sip my espresso in peace but he would have none of that.

The man told me that his name was Arnold and that he had heard of me from a friend of a friend and that I might be in some kind of trouble. I assured him that I certainly wasn't in any kind of trouble and wished him a pleasant evening. He persisted and brought to the table a leather satchel that looked old and weathered. He spoke with an accent that I was unfamiliar with.

“Are you familiar with a dybbuk box, Mr. Kirk?” I shook my head and took another sip – wishing for whiskey. I stared at the bountiful bottom of the waitress near the next table, partly because I was a wretch but mostly because I was trying to remain aloof and not disrespect the poor man currently sitting at my table. He continued. I had no doubt that he would.

“A dybbuk box, Mr. Kirk, is just a box really, fashioned ornately. It is said that a true dybbuk was once a wine cabinet. This I find laughable. All dybbuk boxes are made of wood. No other material will hold it inside.”

“Hold what inside?” I asked – only moderately curious, if anything, to move the conversation along.

“Why, the dybbuk, of course.”

“And what exactly is a dybbuk?” I had to.

“A demon, Mr. Kirk.”

I turned to face him square now. He had my attention. He continued in his foreign drawl – explaining that a dybbuk box is created to capture and hold a demon.

"They are usually red in color and quite old."

"Why are you telling me this, old man?"

"Because you opened yours, didn't you, Walter? You found a box with a boar's head on the clasp. A red box. You knew nothing of what it was so you opened it, didn't you?" He looked around at the various patrons – searching. He lowered his voice. "The creature that encircles you now, Mr. Kirk, is ancient. As old, if not older, than the universe itself. You cannot hope to rid yourself of the creature without first knowing what it wants from you."

All the color had drained from my face and I rested my cup onto the table before I lost its grip in my panic. I needed to lie down. The ground was as good as any a place to rest my head. So, I did just that. Usually after a dream like that, once my head clears, I am able to sleep. This time was no different. I closed my eyes.

In a blink, the vision was gone and I saw that I was signing my name to a document. What a glaringly unsettling feeling. I was at my desk, in my office. The blinds were open to reveal a beautiful summer day.

"Mr. Kirk?"

The ink flowed like water from my pen and I stared down at what I had just put my name to. I had just signed my resignation as a partner with Bricker & Thompson. Why would I do that?

"Mr. Kirk?"

My eyes caught the family photo resting on my desk and I bristled at the sight of Jillian. I remembered. She told me where to find the key. But why? Why do I need to find the key? What did it have to do with these hallucinations? And might it possibly be related to that box that I keep seeing in my nightmares?

"Mr. Kirk, sir?"

I looked up. "Yes, Peter, what can I do for you?" Peter Hastings, my assistant and most valuable asset here at the office. Fresh out of college and he already knew the difference between a cappuccino and a latte. Two extremely marketable skills. As an intern, he was just annoying enough to be tolerable, at times.

"You asked me to come and deliver a letter to Mr. Bricker?"

I looked down at the letter resting on my desk and wondered. I hated it here. Joseph Bricker was a criminal that treated most of his own family like second class citizens. I opened the bottom drawer of my desk and lifted out an envelope, scribbled a couple words on it then folded the letter into it. I held it for a brief moment, looking at my once successful office. I closed many deals right there on those leather chairs. I will regret nothing.

"Here you go, Peter. Have a great rest of your day." I gathered the picture, a golf trophy from last summer, my laptop, and the 9mm Glock I kept in my desk at all times, and exited the office. At the lobby doors, I saw Bricker exit the restroom. He glared at me and I gave him the finger as I pushed happily through the main doors. Freedom's just another word for nothin' left to lose! Thanks, Janice.

Once out and clear from any harm that might befall me at the hands of Joseph Bricker, I phoned James to meet me at Sullivan's for a drink, or perhaps several. It was just what I needed. Sullivan's was our place. It wasn't a bar with its irritating jukebox standards. It was a pub. But not just any pub. Gone are the high stools and wobbly tables. In their place: sofas and coffee tables, lush and comfortable. In the middle of the establishment roared an open fire that, during the holidays, produced freshly roasted chestnuts. It was a glorious place to go and just sit and have a drink. Or several.

"You did what?"

"I signed my resignation."

"Why on earth would you do such a thing? What are you going to do for money?"

I sighed. "First of all, you've known for a very long time, James, that I am in no need of money. I can live off what I have and just be happy and comfortable for the rest of my tormented days." This was, of course, true. When my Uncle Patrick passed away years ago, he left Jillian and I an amount that I am ashamed to reveal. After Jillian's death, and because Uncle Patrick had no children of his own, Jillian's share was absorbed by mine. "Secondly, I can no longer work for that insufferable ass, Joseph Bricker. I don't know how you do it, man."

"Bricker is a puppy dog. Like any dog, you have to give him a treat from time to time."

"Yes, he likes you because you've been getting him laid. He'd certainly have no luck without your help."

It was true. James was on the verge of being terminated only two years ago. A complaint had been logged that James was caught sleeping with a client's wife. This was only a rumor of course, and completely unsubstantiated. However, the very next day, James showed up to work as he usually would. Bricker stormed into his office demanding an explanation. James kept quiet and pulled out his phone and dialed. Within an hour, Bricker was not only sporting a rare smile but James got to keep his job; with a slight increase in pay of course.

I raised my glass to order another round and immediately noticed the blonde across the bar. She was stunningly dressed, not too elegantly for her surroundings in a white blouse that was open just enough to reveal a hidden string of pearls and ample cleavage. Her hair was straight and shimmeringly translucent. She held my gaze and I was arrested by her smile.

"Hey, lover boy?" James brought me back to the land of the living. While my attention was temporarily deterred, he had lined up two shots of his favorite cinnamon flavored liquor. He raised a toast to my misfortune and we downed the warm liquid. My throat caught fire and I gasped at its burning texture. The blonde laughed and I turned back in her direction. She was there and yes, she was laughing, but something was wrong. Something about her had changed. She looked sinister. Her hair appeared wet and matted to her face, a face that suddenly displayed numerous broken bloody wounds. She pointed at me and cackled like an old crow resting wearily on a dirty perch. The room spun and I felt the booze rise with a mixture of bile and humus. I searched quickly for my bag, reached inside and pulled out the cold steel.

Her face turned cold white. Not with fear but more of a natural alteration. I can't tell you why, but I was immediately threatened. Her eyes changed as well; a dark red. No one seemed to notice any of this until I pulled out the gun and pointed the barrel at her head. Even then no one seemed to care that this thing was trying to kill me.

"Walter, have you lost your mind? What the hell are you doing?"

Her face turned cold white

The Glock trembled in my hands and the small number of patrons left had begun to exit. She stood from the bar and strolled in our direction, licking spilled whiskey from the bar top. It's difficult to explain correctly but her face kept changing from this menacing demonic thing back to what I would consider being her normal face, and then just as abruptly, back again. Backing up, I knocked over the stool and there was an explosion as the gun went off in my hand. A dark rosette appeared on the woman's forehead and she stood rigid in place. It was quite unnerving actually. I looked down at the weapon and was shocked to see that it had, in fact, gone off.

The woman still stood, smiling like a doll sitting on an unused bookshelf. Her head tilted dog-like and the smile disappeared. She toppled like an old building, as if her bones had instantly turned to ash in her skin. A vise-like grip took the color from my skin and I looked up to see James staring at me, bewildered. I saw that he was trying to tell me something – yelling, but I couldn't hear him. I seemed to be quite alarmed with my current crisis.

The gun was still warm in my hands and I let go of it and watched as it bounced off the polished oak floor. The woman lay crumpled in a pile of bloodied skin. Steam or possibly smoke billowed from the hole in her head and I stared at it. Fear exuded from my pores and I backed away. The front door was only four feet away and my steps grew wider in stride. The power in the pub went out and the doors automatically locked. The darkness inside seemed infinite. Except for a glowing green orb hovering by the dead body on the floor, there wasn't a single light in the entire place. When he couldn't get my attention after the woman was shot, James hurled a bar stool through the establishment's frosted front window and jumped out, leaving me to my own devices. I can't blame him really. But now, given the current situation, I wished for his guidance, or at least his companionship. Partners in crime, remember?

From the area near or behind the bar resonated a low-frequency hum and the strange green orb hovering above the body grew in size until it was roughly the size of a basketball. I moved in for a closer look but was stopped reluctantly by the voice emanating from the body, still in a pile on the floor.

Hello, Walter. How nice it is to see you.

The voice was not male but neither was it particularly feminine. Underneath the voice was the sound of grinding metal and running water, and again, the sound of forced air.

I wanted to drop by earlier but you seemed busy.

"Do I know you?"

No.

"Why are you here?"

To guide you.

"To guide me? Guide me to what?" I wished that I hadn't dropped the gun.

Let's just say I want to show you something. Something important. Something that I think you should know.

"So, show me."

Before I could change my mind, I was no longer in the dark of the bar. At first, I thought I was flying. I wasn't in the clouds but they were certainly closer than usual. I looked down and saw the bustling city below; about sixty stories below. I was on top of an office building whose top floor was under major construction. There were workers with hammers and drills, welders in goggles, and everywhere were piles of supplies: Sheetrock, wood, and bricks.

"Why am I here?"

Watch your step.

Upon hearing this warning, I looked down and found that I was walking very close to the edge, and I warily tiptoed the precipice – dislodging an already loose brick in the process and sending it tumbling towards the street below. I glanced over the edge in horror, hoping that I hadn't struck an unknowing pedestrian.

Seen enough?

"Seen enough?" I ventured back, confused. "Who are you – the ghost of Christmas stupid?"

The scent of lilac

I found shaking the sudden feeling of suffocation to be extremely difficult, and I was instantly thrust into darkness. It wasn't total and my eyes slowly adjusted. A light panel illuminated to my right and I deduced by that I was in an elevator – not moving. Floors twelve and nine were shining a dull yellow and I smiled sarcastically at my misfortune. Out of twenty-two floors, I have a choice of only two? I chose nine and held my breath as the car moved down two floors and halted abruptly. The doors slid open onto a hallway just as dark and I stepped out. The air was stale but there was the scent of lilac clinging to it, as if someone carrying a fresh bouquet had just passed in front of me. My mother. Despite the lilac, I held my hand up to my face and stepped left down the hall. Garbage and debris littered the dirty carpet and I was forced to navigate a minefield of trash.

In my quick realization, I discovered that the dwellings were laid out in a rectangular pattern and that I was traversing clockwise. Upon the second turn to the right, I was assaulted by the foulest of odors. My first instinct was that of a dead animal. It was certainly not out of the question for an animal to get trapped up here without any possibility of finding nourishment. But then the smell became worse; thicker, as if it were solid – a living thing. I stepped further, using my shirtsleeve as a breathable filter. It seemed to be darker on this stretch, but not too dark for me to notice a person standing directly in the middle of the hall. The features were indiscernible but I was continuing with the assumption that it was a man. Though hidden in complete silhouette, he appeared to move towards me with some struggle and I backed away and drove my legs back to the elevator. A hissing sound was heard and I can't be sure that it wasn't the elevator doors closing but thank goodness they did.

Back inside, I saw that there were different numbers on display this time; seven of them. I searched desperately for the first floor but my hunt was in vain. The closest to it was the third. My idea was to take the stairs from there. Clever enough, right? I pressed the button marked for the third floor and the car shook slightly as it dropped slowly, halting on the floor just slightly above level, causing me to step down. As I did, I was quickly shocked to see that not only was the hallway properly lit but it was clean – devoid of any misuse. Oddly, and in complete contrast to the previous floor, there were people everywhere, coming and going like it was a train station. I searched frantically for the door leading to the stairwell, wanting nothing more than to leave this place. On the third turn, a young woman dressed casually in jeans and an unnaturally tight sweater blocked my progress and addressed me.

"You don't belong here, do you?" asked the woman.

"I'm not exactly sure what you mean," I answered – surprised by the question.

"What I mean exactly is," she looked behind her and then past me. "You're on the wrong floor."

"My thoughts exactly. Would you mind pointing me in the direction of the stairs?"

The young woman seemed to be trembling and I asked quickly if she required assistance – bracing myself for her to pass out right then and there. But she immediately found her composure and instructed me to seek a course back to the elevator and up to the ninth floor.

"But I was just on the ninth floor, and young lady, I do not wish to travel to a higher floor. I simply wish to leave the building.

Might you be able to help me?"

"Oh, wonderful!" She brightened. "Wait, you're not carrying a package?"

"Package? What package? The entire floor was a trash heap."

"You were supposed to obtain a package. My instructions were explicit. There is to be no deviation. You are to turn back to the lift and proceed to the ninth floor. There you will find a package addressed to you. Is this understood?"

"I'm sorry, but I believe you have me mistaken for someone else. I just want to leave the building and go home. It's been a horribly long day and all of this elevator business has been quite taxing. Now, if you wouldn't mind, please show me to the stairs."

The ground beneath me shook, and for a moment I lost my balance and teetered slightly, catching myself on the wall to my left. The girl though, she stood firm – staring at me through eyes half covered by lids pancaked in blue glitter. Cracks appeared in the ceiling's plaster and I worried that I would be trapped in this hell, having no one to talk to other than this – girl. After a few moments of panic, the floor steadied and I was returned upright. Again, she looked behind her and I used this as an opportunity to move past her, but she had anticipated my subterfuge and caught me by the shoulders and whispered to me with a voice so soft and so uncomfortably sensual that my muscles became as gelatin and I felt movement between my legs. Some other time perhaps.

"Walter, please listen to me carefully. You are to proceed to the ninth floor where you will retrieve a package. Once you have the package you will be able to leave the building as you desire. If you refuse to accept the package, you will not be allowed access out of the building. Do we have an understanding? Yes? Good. Go."

Once out from under her spell, I entered the elevator as instructed but I refused to take orders from a heavy chested twenty-something. I was not going back to the ninth floor. In contrast to her orders, the ninth floor was not even illuminated. This time I was given only one choice: the twentieth floor. I sighed in frustration and pressed the yellow button, only the elevator did not move. Not a fan of elevators, I should have felt a sudden lurch in my gut as the car was hoisted upward but there was nothing. A faint bell dinged as the doors once again slid open.

I stepped out onto old tiled flooring that resonated with each step. There were people all around me: everywhere; in all directions, moving swiftly with purpose but the intense white light from above me was making it extremely difficult to focus on anything or anyone. I ran to the nearest visible door, entered the room and closed it behind me. There was a dense fog or a mist that only exacerbated the extreme light.

I searched for something to sit on and was overjoyed to find a cheap yellow leather sofa. I took off my shoes and fell back onto the cracked leather. It may have been plastic or even vinyl. It mattered little. I needed to rest and refocus not only my weary body but my troubled mind. And so, I did. I had never felt so comfortable on something so uncomfortable before. I was thankful that I had found it, but my mind continued to search out answers to questions it knew nothing about. Who was that girl on the third floor? How does she know me? And what was this mysterious package that I was to recover?

My eyes closed and I attempted a shutdown, if only for a short while. An hour. Please? Before I felt the icy hand on my forehead a voice spoke from across the room.

"Walter." The room sounded hollow and empty but the sound

of machines informed me otherwise. “Are you alright?”

My lids opened instantly and I tried to look past the fog to where the voice was coming from. It was a little more than a whisper but I knew that it was my dad. His voice was soft yet scratchy – a smoker’s cough. He gently placed his worn dry hand on my head in an attempt to comfort me. I wasn’t comforted. Perhaps he felt this because he withdrew his hand as quickly as he had put it there.

“Dad?” I heard him cry.

“You’re going to be just fine, son. You just need to wake up.”

“But, Dad, I’m not asleep.”

“I know that, son.” I heard him shuffling around beyond the mist like he was pacing – working through a problem. That was my dad alright. Whenever he was faced with a problem, or some crisis either from work or at home, you can guarantee that he would pace the floor of his office until he came to a solution. Oftentimes that solution would not come to him for days, and the pacing would continue. I remember one night when I was little. He had left his office door open and I watched him move about the room, from behind his large desk to out in front of it, then back again. If he were to stop or sit, it would only be for a second or two, then the pacing would continue until he yelled, "I've got it!" Then the pacing would cease until the next crisis arose. "I need you to do me a favor."

"What kind of favor?"

I heard his shoes echo on the hard tile floor and sensed that he was walking towards me. I closed my eyes and felt his breath on my face as he whispered in my ear.

"Release me."

"I don't understand, Dad."

"Release me. I have been stuck in that house for almost thirty years now. I can't leave, and I have to exist through a replay of the night your sister and I were murdered. It replays every night. Over and over and over; for eternity."

"How am I supposed to stop that? What do you want me to do?"

He whispered again but this time it was harder to hear

"Retrieve the package." I sat up quickly and came face to face with my father. He looked better than I thought he might. There was no flaky skin that is usually associated with people who are supposed to be dead. I shook my head and resolved to the task.

"Dad, why did Mom kill you and Jillian?" There was a jumble of words that I couldn't understand and Dad's face changed. He looked sad. Well, in truth, he looked sad before but he looked so beaten down. He said more incoherent words and then fell back into the mist. I was disappointed that he didn't answer but I stood and wiped my tears on my sleeve. Outside the room was still as blinding but I felt my way back to the elevator, and wouldn't you know it, floor nine was available this time. How convenient.

Once again, the smell burned my eyes and I traveled around all the broken pieces of life. Waste and refuse were slowly absorbed by the already molded flooring. I had the sickening feeling that the man that I had left up here before was holding this package that I was to recover. Instead of walking the entire network, I took a left from the elevator and saw the creature just around the first corner. A man? Yes. However, he was covered in what looked at first to be scales – black, greasy fish scales - and as I got closer, I had no cause to believe otherwise. A black top hat sat upon a head covered in stringy black hair, just as greasy as the rest of his odd-looking body. If I didn't know better, I would say that the man suffered from shingles, but a case this severe would not allow a person to be mobile, let alone stand in one spot for very long. I took another step closer and his head snapped in my direction. A hideous snarl graced his hideous face and he opened his snake-like mouth to speak, but what was spoken I was unable to comprehend. If I had to describe it I would call it gibberish. I nodded, pretending to understand, and the thing turned and picked up a parcel, wrapped in shipping tape. He threw it to the floor next to him and kicked it over to me. I was extremely thankful that I wasn't required to move any closer to him.

I snatched the package with haste and spun on my heals in the direction of the elevator. A creature, looking the same as the other, blocked me from continuing. When I protested, I was spat upon with bloody puss and I gagged, dropped to my knees and clawed at my throat. I let loose a scream and felt a sudden urge to vomit but was left with nothing but a dry lurch.

Laughter, evil, tormented laughter split my head open from the inside and I was sure I would go mad. It echoed down the hall that no longer seemed like a hall but more like a tunnel. A tunnel of brain matter and gore. Entrails hung from the walls and ceiling like

Spanish moss at an antebellum plantation. Eyes glared at me through the greasy bloody walls. As I stepped through the tunnel, hands riddled with open sores grabbed at my ankles and tried to pull me down. I screamed again and they ceased for only a moment and I was back in the elevator before I knew it.

The lift took me, unbelievably, all the way down to the parking level. It was not an ideal landing but it was certainly preferable to the ninth or even the third floor. It was dark, illuminated dimly with red exit signs. I followed the signs and exited the building through a large metal door, carrying the package under my arm.

Believe me when I say that I understand completely just how strange this sounds but I heard the package speak to me. I was unclear as to what it was saying exactly but the compulsion to open it was too great not to find the nearest bench and sit down. I spotted a park to the north of the building I had exited. The sun was beating down upon me like a hammer and I took a path through the park. All around me was life and I felt a modicum of comfort. Even if I had gone mad, the rest of the world was still moving along despite me.

Marty, you were right

1978

Jillian and Walter sat together on the front lawn as the police officers questioned their parents. Neighbors looked on in curiosity. A kind female officer had talked to both of them together and then separately. From what Jillian had learned, Aunt Bethany had gone missing and there was a suicide note left behind.

At approximately 2:30 the previous morning, Marty had walked into the kitchen to find his sister in law sitting at the kitchen table, a half empty bottle of Wild Turkey lovingly held between her legs. Her hair was wet and she looked as if she had been crying.

"Bethany?" He asked her quietly, "What happened to you? Where have you been?"

Three hours before, Bethany and her sister had gotten into a terrible argument regarding Bethany's decision not to quit drinking. Beatrice had told her that if she was going to be around the children then there was to be no more drinking. Bethany stormed out of the house claiming that she would be back the next day for her belongings, only to return a few hours later, drunk and nowhere to go. He snatched the bottle from her and poured it down the drain.

"Go get some sleep. You and Bea will work this out in the morning." Marty started towards the steps and stopped. Perhaps it was because he had become accustomed to her being around and seeing her with the kids, he suddenly felt sorry for her. He looked back.

"Beth." She looked up at him. "Don't let Beatrice or the kids see you like this."

The next morning, Beatrice had gotten up early and trudged down the stairs for coffee. She noticed a single sheet of notebook paper placed in the middle of the table on purpose. She held it up to her face to read it. Without her glasses it was a little blurry but readable.

Bea, I'm sorry. I'm so sorry for not being the sister that you deserved all those years ago. I was never a good person. I wanted to be, or I think I wanted to be, but Dad took any happiness away from me. And now I realize that I can never be truly happy. I don't want to be in your way any longer. I am so sick and tired of being sorry. I need to take responsibility for my actions. One day, when we meet together in the afterlife, I hope you can forgive me. Tell the children that I love them.

Marty, you were right. You were always right.

Beatrice took in a deep breath, closed her eyes and counted to five, then flung herself up the stairs, calling for her husband along the way.

The police had found no trace of Bethany, nor was there any evidence of foul play. There was only the note that she had left behind. The note never mentioned suicide so the police never investigated. If she had killed herself, how did she do it? Who writes a suicide note then packs all of their belongings and leaves? That was surely strange and the kind female officer told the kids that if she heard anything about their aunt she would tell them. But if she didn't kill herself, then there was no crime for the police to investigate.

Jillian sat in the grass next to her brother Walter and watched her mother as she spoke to the same female officer. She seemed relaxed – almost calm. The female officer looked back at Jillian and smiled. Her mother, however, lit a cigarette and blew the smoke over her head. She laughed at something the officer had said. Jillian's skin prickled and she grabbed Walter's hand.

All around me was life

Children ran – chasing each other and laughing while parents, single or otherwise, walked dogs, and peddled bicycles. Fitness junkies jogged in place and guzzled water from clear plastic bottles. Families ate barbeque from picnic tables covered in red and white checkered tablecloths. I ached to be one of them, to no longer be held within this state of walking death. Just once to be among them, to live my life as it once was. Just once. To once again walk within the light of the sun rather than in its shadow. To laugh with friends and embrace with passion. Penelope. My dear sweet Penelope. Was she gone now forever?

At a junction was a fountain. Along its sides were ornate concrete benches. I took my rest upon one of these, facing a father and son tossing a flying disc back and forth to each other. I sighed and smiled as I tore the wrappings from the package. The contents of the package sent the smile on my face running for shelter. I set aside the wrapping next to me and held the thing in my hands. It was all too familiar, though I strained to recall how. It was a box, a jewelry box I believe. Wooden, with polished brass fittings. An animal of some type adorned the clasp and a lock was held from its mouth. The box itself was stained an eerie red. Crimson if you ask me. And it smelled old. The weight was substantial though upon lifting it I concluded that it held nothing inside. Though the lock was clearly holding the lid in place, I lifted the box open easily. Inside was a torn piece of notebook paper. It was the same paper that was in Jillian's notebook diary. I plucked it out of the box and turned it over. I tilted my head like a curious dog at the cryptic message written in my sister's handwriting.

Walter, open the box. Quickly.

I looked around me at the activity – conscious that I was being watched from somewhere. Hadn't I always been watched? Instantly, I gathered the box and the wrappings and left the park – traveling north alongside a busy street. A sensation of sheer terror invaded my mind and I stole a glance behind me. I was being followed. A man, dressed in clothes meant to be ignored. And yet I spotted him right away. He wore jeans, torn at one knee. A sports jersey of some type with a matching hat placed backward upon shoulder length blonde curls. At first glance, it looked like he was carrying something. His hands deep in his pockets and I stiffened in reaction. I stopped at a storefront and watched him pass behind me. I was possibly overreacting. It wouldn't be the first time.

I continued north, looking all around me – paranoid as a dope fiend – and swallowed hard when I saw the man walking toward me. I instantly stiffened noticeably. He passed me on my left then turned to step up behind me as I crossed an intersection outside a popular bookshop. He grasped my arm and led me through the throng of people, bustling in the hot summer sun. I was dizzy with fear.

"Do not be afraid of me, Walter," he told me – loud enough for those around to hear.

"Who are you?" I kept walking without looking in his direction.

"My name is Michael, and I am not here to harm you, Walter. I am here to help you. But you must listen to me and you must do as I say. Do you understand?"

I did not answer him at first. I didn't hear him, or maybe I didn't want to hear him.

"Do you understand?"

I nodded in agreement but was reluctant to trust anyone so I agreed but kept my guard up.

He guided me through the mass of movement, the exodus of comings and goings. In and out of stores and shops; clothing and electronic gadgets, books and galleries. We passed a florist whose door was open and I was hit by a wave of lilac and I was stunned by the sensation that my mother had been here recently. But that's not possible.

"I see that you got my package." He motioned at the box under my arm but I did not answer. "Walter, it's important that you understand what that is. You must keep it safe."

"And what is it?"

"The answer to that question will come to you soon enough, but I can tell you this…" He stopped at a corner and looked out at the park that I was sitting in less than an hour ago. There was a distant look in his eyes like he was there but somewhere else at the same time. "The answer to all of you questions are here." He poked at my head. “Right here.”

“I don’t understand.” I dropped down on to a bus stop bench, frustrated. “What is this box? What does it have to do with me? What am I doing here?”

This last question hit home rather quickly because I was overtaken by a sudden feeling of vertigo. No, that’s not exactly true. I can’t be certain what it’s called but I was lost. I didn’t know where I was. Not just mentally or emotionally but physically. I had no idea where I was. Michael looked up into a clear blue sky. His mouth was moving as if he was praying. It was an odd scene. He then wiped a bead of sweat from his brow and came to sit next to me on the bench.

“Where you are, Walter, is not as important as where you are in here.” He poked my head again in reference to my mind I was assuming. “Once you’re awake, all of this, all of these questions will be answered and you will understand. But, Walter, you must wake up. Wake up, Walter.”

Wake up Walter.

"Wake up? What do you mean, wake up? Am I not awake?

"How about we get a bite to eat. I love hot dogs. Are you hungry?" He slapped my knee and stood, surveying the local food offerings.

"I'm not hungry. I'll stay right here, thank you very much."

"Okay, suit yourself."

And just like that, he was gone and I rolled over and stared at the glowing red numbers of my alarm clock: 2:22 AM. Why couldn't I sleep? Yes, I know, I have a lot on my mind, and I rarely sleep as it is these days. I had a deadline to keep to – my report to Bricker on the Williamsburg case. It was driving me mad. A client had come across a number of documents relating to the Founding Fathers. So far, all efforts to validate the documents have been unsuccessful. If they were what the client claimed they were, they may end up being very valuable. My next move was to call in a favor, this of course was the last thing that I wanted to do because Randy and I were no longer on speaking terms. Randall Hostetler was the most notable archivist in Washington. Upon receipt, he would run a number of tests to ensure their validity. From there he would run a trace on former ownership. If the previous owner was no longer among the living with no living heirs, the client would be awarded ownership. The problem was that Randy hated my guts, and trust me the feeling was mutual.

For the simple sake of moving this along, I will tell you about Randall P. Hostetler. It was nothing as cliché as we were school chums or college buddies. No, it's much less complicated. I was interning for Craig Mueller while studying for the Bar examine – this is not as glamorous as it sounds. Interning for a respectable attorney is about as glamorous as sweeping up peanut shells in one of those ridiculous steakhouse chains. Making coffee and copying papers were my most exhausting tasks. On one particular morning, I had a number of presentations from Mr. Mueller that needed to get to the printer and back the very next day and, of course, I was running late. The binders were stacked neatly in a cardboard box and I was hurrying back to the office with them when out comes this boisterous brute from a coffee shop on my left. To say that he bumped into me would be the understatement of the millennium. He literally barreled into me like a running back, like a pit bull suddenly let loose after a chipmunk. The box was crushed and the presentations, all thirty-five of them, went hurtling through the air, landing in the nearest puddle of slush.

My life flashed before my eyes in a splash of snowy ice and I fell to my knees in hopes of finding a dry one. I turned up to him. Apparently, I had spilled his coffee. There were plenty of 'what the hell's and 'how could you's. It was not my initial intention to engage in a physical altercation with the monster but I was incensed. Three weeks of hard, grueling work destroyed. Yes, of course, the printer would have copies of the original files but it would be another twenty-four hours. Mr. Mueller needed them that afternoon. I stood. Moved closer to him; ready to strike.

"Thanks for spilling my coffee, dick!" That was all he said, then stomped off up the street to only God knows where. I was left there feeling like a fool with a handful of wet, nearly disintegrated paper. The graphs, full color, were ruined. Expense reports that I alone put together, destroyed. I had to walk the lonely mile back to the office and explain to my boss that the presentations that I promised him would be ready on that day were not ready. I would surely be fired. My Bar examine was in two weeks. I wanted to go back there and find that guy and put a knife to his throat. But alas, that was not me. I was correct in assuming that I would be fired. I was made to clear out my desk that afternoon. Lawyers are merciless on the weak.

Once I became a full partner at Bricker and Associates, I was able to secure more meaningful cases for myself, ones that dealt with sensitive situations. Because of this, I was given access to the chief archivist at the National Archives in Washington. His name: Randall Hostetler, the same jerk that bowled me over so many years ago. So, you can understand my reluctance.

My life flashed before my eyes

Another roll to the left: 3:07 am. What was the point? I threw my feet off the bed and stood on the cold wood floor. Why had I chosen wood flooring? The white light burned my eyes at the sink and I splashed some cold water on my face to assist in the morning motivation. It wouldn't be the first time that I would be at the office so early. As a matter of fact, wasn't it just the other day? But this was the earliest. I was dressed and out on the street by four but by the time I reached for the keys I felt a sudden rush of air, and it seemed odd that the sun was rising so early. I made the attempt to enter the car but was caught by a voice, the same voice I had heard many times. I was compelled to ignore it when my throat began to throb and there was a stinging sensation in both wrists and I fell back on to the pavement, and for some strange reason, I was overcome with the urge to vomit.

"Walter, can you hear me?"

I spun around – looking for the voice that was just in my ear but there was nobody there. It seemed as though I was being poked and prodded. My nerves were active like never before and I felt a pain on the top of my head.

"Walter!"

The light from the sun was brighter now and I covered my eyes to see but as soon as I did, the imagery before me changed. It was out of focus for certain but definitely different. And the perspective was erroneously skewed. If I hadn't known better, I would have bet that I was on my back. Had I fallen again? I looked around for my car but was greeted by an entirely off-putting scenario.

"Look! He's opening his eyes. Run and get the doctor. Quickly!" It was the same voice that had called my name just moments ago. The voice I had known for quite some time. The voice of my best friend James. But it was no longer just a voice. He was there, standing over me. There were others as well, and the light was like a laser beam cauterizing my retinas. I tried to speak but was unable to find my voice. I brought my hands up to cover my face from the light.

“Penelope, would you turn those lights off, please?” It was still James. Something was terribly wrong. I struggled to speak but my throat forbade me any attempt. “Don’t try to talk, Walter. You’re gonna be just fine.”

The light had eventually dimmed and my focus was returning slowly. I was on my back on a bed, this I was sure of. The room I was in though confused me. I kept looking back to my right, expecting to see my apartment building, but it appeared that I was no longer standing on Herald Circle. And then it was all too obvious. A tall man, sporting a full beard and square-rimmed glasses entered the room. He spoke to James – speaking words that I was unable to hear or understand. He was carrying a clipboard and stepped closer to the side of the bed that I was lying on. He wore a white coat. His name was Paul. He was my doctor. I was in a hospital.

“Mr. Kirk. Can you hear me?”

I nodded my acknowledgment.

“My name is Paul Fox. I’m a doctor. Do you remember me?”

I shook my head slowly. I did not remember him. How could I? I didn’t remember anything. No, that’s not true. I remembered everything. Every single detail of the last few days. I trembled in terror – afraid that my nightmares had finally taken their toll and put me in the hospital. I opened my mouth again. This time a whisper was successful.

"Why am I here?"

James stepped forward, excusing the doctor from the uncomfortable explanation. "Walter, you were involved in an accident." I cringed and immediately thought of my car. Had I totaled it? Had I hurt someone else? James picked up on my internal turmoil. "It wasn't a car accident or anything like that. You were hit by a brick that had fallen from the top of the Crichton Building. You're lucky to be alive."

That last statement hit me as hard as I could imagine the brick had hit me and I felt warm tears pool. I reached up and studied my head with my fingers. IV lines were attached to both arms. My eyesight was rapidly improving and I groaned as I glanced about the room. For a hospital room, it appeared quite tech-heavy. There were machines on all but one wall – displaying red numbers and green numbers, peaks, and valleys. Three separate printers spewed out tiny rolls of data. The doctor made notes from all three.

I looked back up at James and presented him with the best smile I could muster. He smiled back, but his smile betrayed an amount of sadness. Clearly, there was more of the story and my pleading look bade him to go on.

"There's something else, Walter." See, I told you. "You know that the Crichton Building is like sixty floors high right? I mean, we all thought you were gone. You didn't even have a pulse when they brought you here." I squinted my eyes slightly as if to tell him that I didn't understand.

"Maybe this isn't the right time." That voice was female and out of my line of sight. I didn't recognize it either. I looked around the room – searching for the female that owned the voice. James stepped aside and I was greeted with the prettiest smile I had ever seen; apart from my mother, of course. But who she was, I did not know. She looked comfortable in a white blouse and tan slacks. But what struck me the most about her appearance was the shimmering string of pearls around her slender neck and I quickly knew who she was.

"Penelope?" I whispered. I assumed that she would never want to see me again after what had happened.

"Hello, Walter." She smiled and held my hand. The doctor appeared again at my side and I looked at both of them. What was I missing?

"What's going on?" I asked. It was the doctor that spoke.

"Mr. Kirk, the injury you sustained caused severe trauma to your brain. Substantial hemorrhaging caused a subdural hematoma. We relieved the pressure and prevented any permanent damage to the brain but," he paused here. "The injury put you in a coma."

The word sounded foreign. In all of my life, I had never – that I can recall – knew anyone that was in or had been in a coma. My mind went through all the reasons that I could tell this man that he was wrong. I had not been in a coma. I had been suffering from some really messed up dreams but a coma? Hell no. What about the girl that I had shot? James would remember that. And Debra, yes, what about Debra? Call Debra. She will tell you that I was there.

I had not been in a coma. Had I? I shook my head in complete disagreement.

"What's the last thing you remember?" James asked me.

"Walking to my car to go to work this morning."

“Anything else?” Yes, but I wasn’t about to confess to the things that my disturbed mind was making me believe was real. So I shook my head. James smiled again. I was glad he was here.

“Do you remember Jackie?” I thought hard and found that name tucked away.

“Yes, you took me to Sullivan’s to meet her. Right?” Was that the girl I shot?

“That’s right, Walter. It was then that you got hit. The brick fell on your head when you got out of the car. I called 911 and followed the ambulance here.”

I felt my head once again and struggled to recall the accident. I looked up at the doctor whose face confirmed what James was telling me. I couldn’t hold back the gnawing question that confronted me the moment the word coma was spoken. I’m sure you’ve been wondering the same thing. I have been too afraid to ask – not wanting to know the answer – not wanting to know the truth about my condition.

“How long have I been gone?”

“Walter.” A frown painted the face of my best friend.

"How long?"

"It's not important, Walter. What's important is that you're going to be alright."

My eyes were open wide and in full focus. I wanted to sit up but was too weak. All I could manage to do was prop my dizzy body up onto my elbows.

"How long, James?"

"A year," he said sadly. "A year and two months to be exact."

My elbows dropped. I became upset – agitated. So much so that the nurses came in to sedate me. My mind, in the state that it was in, was not able to comprehend the severity of this. I had been in a coma for over a year. During that time I had lost thirty-seven pounds even though I had been fed intravenously. My hair had grown and a beard adorned my face.

A Year?

After that day, I had to endure a number of months of physical therapy to rebuild my atrophied muscles. It was grueling but I have to tell you being rid of the nightmares was all the pleasure that I required. James and I were back to our old shenanigans. He finally introduced me to Jackie, who was now his fiancé. There's a shocker if I ever heard one. I called Debra one evening and was relieved to learn that she was alive and well – still living in Middleton, with a man now. I'm still not sure how I feel about that but I'll get over it I'm sure. Penelope and I – so I learned – were to have our first date on the night of my accident, set up by James himself. So, because I was in a coma and unable to attend the date, she forgave me and we rescheduled. So far we are getting along quite well and are looking forward to seeing each other more often. I was happy to feel normal again but my life had changed and would never be the same as before. I became more aware of my surroundings. I drove safer. I was more careful with my life. I realize that it sounds funny but life truly is a precious and fragile thing. I almost lost mine and I didn't want to ever go through that feeling again.

I left the firm and opened my own practice outside the city. New clients were pouring in and I was starting to make a new name for myself. This spurred the eventual move from the apartment in the circle to an actual home. I even gave up the sports car for something a bit more practical and economical. I planted a garden in the backyard and taught myself how to cook. These were truly happy times. Penelope and I continued to enjoy the warm weather. September was still hot and she would often bring her dog Dixie over when she visited, an American Bulldog whom I loved. It was one of these nights roughly three weeks ago that we went for a walk around the neighborhood. We met Joe and Susan Shilt. Joe is a web designer of some talent and Susan is a behavioral psychologist with the US Government. Very hush hush. Then there was Fred and Nancy Ritter – an older retired couple who decided to walk with us for a stretch. Fred was a veteran of the Korean War with a Purple Heart. He met Nancy on the plane coming home from the war. She was a flight attendant who had tripped and fell into Fred's lap. They fell in love almost instantly.

After Fred and Nancy turned back home, we met Blake and

Justin, a gay couple who had just recently moved to the neighborhood. They made us laugh harder than we had in quite some time. Justin was a teacher and Blake flipped houses for a living. They were dressed in the most outrageous clothes. I covered a laugh with a throat clearing and Penelope gave me an elbow to the ribs.

"You should see my latest design," Blake exclaimed proudly. "It's not far, just over on Berkshire." The street name took me by surprise. "4237 is the address if you get over there. Kind of an older home, but it certainly had potential. Wanna see it?"

Penelope squeezed my hand to comfort me and told the boys no thank you, we would take a look at it some other time.

"I'm sure it's lovely though," she told them. But I had something different in mind.

"Sure, let's go see it. I love those house flipping shows. Don't you, honey?" I squeezed her hand back and walked a few more blocks north, led by Blake and Justin who talked about their twin Pekinese puppies the entire way there. It was humorous but slightly annoying.

Welcome home, Walter... Again

We turned the corner on to Berkshire and I felt a turn in the pit of my stomach. The grass was greener than any lawn a man could dream of. It was lush and thick yet soft as a pillow. The house itself looked nothing like I remembered and I remarked to Penelope that this was not the home of my once troubled childhood. The dingy old white siding that I remember had been replaced by a grayish blue clapboard. It was definitely an upgrade.

"You guys wanna see inside? I got the keys." I nodded. Penelope was worried – knowing as much of the history of this house as anyone, she was concerned that I was going too far too quickly, but she stood by me. "I need to do this," I whispered to her.

"Let's do it." I hoped that I hadn't sounded too enthusiastic. As much as I wanted to see the house, I had mixed emotions. These two, though they had good intentions, had no idea what had happened here. If they knew that both my father and my sister were both murdered here, by my mother who then killed herself, I think they would leave and never return – after emptying their stomachs, of course.

Blake pulled a ring of keys from his pocket and opened the front door. A fresh smell of cedar hit my nose and I was taken back by how different the place appeared. It was my home yes, but with a vague layout and a modern twist. Gone were the gaudy shag carpeting and dreadful wallpaper. Hardwood and granite decorated everything in a black & tan kind of feel. It was the kind of home that would proudly grace the pages of many home magazines. And though it was remodeled, I knew where everything was. What I mean is, I knew where to look and I began to hatch my plan. To get what I wanted required a little honesty. Penelope was still concerned about me. As was I. I was not prepared for this.

"Hey, guys," I called to them as Blake was describing the advanced appliances in the kitchen. "I have a confession to make." They both looked at me with child-like interest. "This is not the first time that I've been inside this house." The look of interest on Blake's face turned to concern automatically. His head tilted like a curious canine. He stepped closer and leaned against the granite countertop – a median of blankness.

Justin answered for his partner. “What do you mean?”

“I was born in this house. It’s my childhood home. That kitchen where you’re standing in is the room where I took my first steps.” In honor, I took a step forward. “Right here is where the kitchen table stood – where I would eat breakfast and dinner, and after school, I did my homework here while my mother watched.” She always watched.

At first I thought that they would be annoyed. Why hadn’t I told them this before we entered? What was I up to? This was not the case. They seemed to really love the idea and I got the impression that they were hoping that I would buy it from them. I really couldn’t care less about this place. It reminded me of times that I would rather forget. But I didn’t want them to know that so it was up to me to lay it on thick to them. I turned towards the front room and was able to bring up a tear or two.

“This is where my father would sit and read his paper every evening – with me sitting longingly at his feet.” One more round.

This time by the front window. I actually stopped and looked at the floor. "While sitting in this spot, I remember my mother telling me that she loved me. I'm sure she had said it many times before." I knelt down and graced the floor with the palm of my hand. "I remember her saying it here for the first time."

I needed to move quickly if I were going to get this done. Penelope looked at me with a quizzical expression. I didn't have time to explain to her what my plan was because I didn't know of it until it was too late. I had almost wished that this didn't go down this way but I didn't have a choice. My path was laid out in front of me and I went for it.

"Would you guys allow me a few minutes in here alone? Just to simply reminisce with my past and take a walk through the bedrooms?" My attempt at the perfect sad kitty face must've worked because before I could even continue the explanation, they told me that they would be outside waiting and for us to take our time. Jackpot!

I took Penelope by the wrist and led her up the stairs. At the top I paused. Was that lilac? No. It was. I hadn't seen any fresh sprigs. It was impossible. The first door at the top of the stairs was

Jillian's room and I pushed the door open. The color drained from my face. The room was nothing like I had remembered it. It bore no resemblance whatsoever and I wondered if I was in the correct room. I knew that I was but I questioned my memory.

"We should hurry, Walter. Where did she leave it?"

Penelope's words shook me out of me revere and I charged the closet like a base runner heading for home plate. It was empty of course, but to get what I had come for I would have to cause a bit of damage. Inside the closet, as she told me, there was a hole on the left wall towards the bottom, near the trim, and using my knuckles I knocked around to find the sweet spot. It didn't take long.

"Pass me your car keys, my dear." Penelope reached into her purse and retrieved her keys. It was a long shot but If I could dig a hole into the drywall using a key as a saw, I might be able to find it with minimal harm. This was not as successful as I had anticipated, however, and the hole I created in the process was considerable – wide enough for my entire hand. I reached in and searched; nothing. I pushed in further; nothing.

"Could it be that you're in the wrong spot?"

"Not a chance, darling. It's here. Just a few more seconds and I'll have it."

A few more seconds became uncomfortable as the time ticked passed a minute, then two. Sweat had gathered on my brow and down the back of my neck and Penelope rushed over to the window. Blake and Justin appeared to be quite content smoking out on the front lawn. Three minutes. But when Penelope got up to look again they were walking towards the front door, checking their watches and appearing anxious.

"Walter," she whispered frantically. "They're coming. Please hurry."

I reached my arm in as far as it would go but I only came up with dust. Stretching to the right, I felt a mass of hard aluminum duct work that had obviously been installed when the house was new. I exhaled and pushed in to the right. I felt something brush my fingertips.

"Got it!" My hand fell upon a wrapped canvas package sealed with packing tape, no bigger than a Post-it, and I pulled it out and quickly pocketed it. I stood and we hastily exited the house, greeting the gleeful couple as they were just climbing the stairs.

"Thanks, fellas. I greatly appreciate you allowing me to do that."

"Oh, not a problem at all." Justin smiled. "We're happy to help."

"I suppose that I needed a bit of closure."

A key to what?

We all shook hands and the party was over. We escorted the gentlemen back down the block and back home. It took Penelope and I exactly four minutes to run back to my house and lock the front door. I whisked a pair of scissors from a kitchen drawn and attacked the old paper without any hesitation. It was held together with clear tape that fell apart quite easily. Once I had one side open, the item slid out onto the kitchen table and we both sat there staring – in realization that my vision was real. Jillian told me where the key was and it was actually there. It was brass for sure but old and tarnished.

The bow was in the shape of an oval, and it looked as though there were teeth marks on the stem and the pin. The bit was intact, however. Thank goodness for that.

“So, now what?” Penelope asked. It was a valid question. What, indeed.

“I haven’t the slightest idea, darling, but I can’t imagine that a magnificent steak would trouble our efforts any.”

"That does sound good," she said, standing. "But let's not go to Randolph's."

She smiled at me in spite of the terrible story I told her and we opened the door to leave. The key was safe, on a chain around my neck. A thin blonde woman with an athletic build greeted us at the door. She was wearing a dark brown uniform – shorts with steel-toe sneakers.

"Walter Kirk?" she asked, holding an electronic device.

I nodded and was asked to sign a bulky electric clipboard. After which I was handed a package. Large, roughly the size of a hat box. It was not heavy but there was substance. The package was addressed to me with an unknown sender.

"Have a great day!" she yelled, already halfway to the box truck parked in front of the house, painted the same color brown as her uniform.

Penelope and I chose to forego our dinner plans, for the moment at least, and focus on the package. I must say truthfully that it reminded me of the package I was forced to retrieve from that office building during my dark time. It was certainly the same size and shape. This realization forced me to place the box down on the floor and take a step back. My mind raced through all the moments that I had encountered the thing. Yes, I know; I was in a coma and dreaming but that doesn't mean that it felt any less real to me. The fear that I felt while I was unconscious for so long was real, and I find myself from time to time worrying that my life as it exists now could be just another manifestation of all that horror that my mind created. Penelope sure does do her best at ensuring me that my life is real, that my reality is real. She has been a true source of inspiration for me and I will forever remain in her debt. Yes, of course, I was being ridiculous. I stepped forward and hauled the thing over to the couch and employed the scissors once again, carefully removing the paper and bubble wrap.

My hands shook as I revealed the contents. The color drained from my face as a red wooden box came into focus. Penelope grabbed my arm and we exchanged looks of frightened bewilderment.

"This can't be happening. This can't be real," I said as Penelope pinched my arm.

"Don't worry, honey," she comforted. "You're real."

The object was just as I remembered it – just as my visions remembered it. It was roughly the size of an average jewelry box. The hinges and fittings were of polished brass. The wood was high quality, stained red but allowing the grain to shine through. On the front, the first thing noticeable was a rusted out lock that looked to be considerably old. The shape of the keyhole was familiar. Behind it was the clasp – hideous in shape – a boar's head. It was as if it were staring right through me.

"What does this mean?" asked Penelope. I lifted the key from around my neck.

"There's only one way to find out, my dear." I entered the key into the old lock and twisted. At first, it resisted and the key moved not at all. But after a third attempt, the key turned and the rusty innards clicked rather loudly and the lock fell open. From the looks of it, the lock had never been opened before.

I carefully opened the lid. Just as Jillian had mentioned in her diary, the lid creaked like a casket. Slowly, we both peered over the top and looked inside. To our astonishment, there was nothing terrible waiting. At least not at first glance. As we allowed our stomachs to settle from the initial shock, we saw that resting on the plush velvet were two sealed envelopes and a folded note. The envelopes were official, meaning that they were from the courthouse. They were addressed to no one but the seal was stamped on the front and back of both.

The note, on the other hand, was quite an interesting piece of archaeology. It was written by my Uncle Mark. As I read the words out loud, I felt my arms go numb, then my entire body was weak as I was confronted with a revelation more astounding then my mind was able to fathom.

Let me start by putting you at ease

Dear Jillian & Walter,

If you are reading this then I am dead and it is finally time for you to know the truth about your mother. Let me start by putting you at ease. Your mother was a wonderful woman. She took care of the two of you better than I've ever known a mother to do so – better than our own mother that's for sure. As a wife, I'm not as certain but I never knew your father to be unhappy. More than this; she was my best friend, and that's not an easy thing to say. She was always there for me when I needed someone.

Now, for the bad news: the woman that you believe to be your mother, is not your mother. Your real mother; the woman that gave birth to the two of you, died when you were both 5 and 7 years old. She was killed by our sister; her twin sister Bethany. I realize that this is going to be a shock, just as it was when I made the connection. Beth murdered your mother out of jealousy. It's just as simple as that. She wanted a life that she could never achieve, so she killed her own sister for it. She was evil when we were kids and she is evil now.

A number of years ago Bethany went missing and I was certainly happy to learn that she might never come home. It was thought that she found a man, got married and chose to leave her family. Mom and Dad waited for years and years but she never returned.

Something was off though when I would come over to visit her and the two of you, she seemed distant and well, just not herself. She had taken up drinking which was not like her at all. But the final straw for me was when I went to our parents' house and started snooping through Bethany's things that they had kept after her disappearance. In a shoe box that she had marked private, I found a bracelet. It was cheap and flimsy but she wore it all the time. It was inscribed with: To Beatrice. How do I know about this? I bought her the bracelet for her birthday when we were just kids. She loved it and told me that she would never take it off.

Trust me, kids, when I say that your mother is not your mother. She is your aunt Bethany. You may remember her as your first nanny, it's true. Your mother and her sister reunited briefly, but only so that she could kill her and take you kids as her own. She is pure evil and will do anything to keep the life that she stole. Stay away from her if you can.

I've sent along both Bethany's and your Mother's birth certificates for proof. I have also given you the bracelet. Don't let her see it.

Uncle Mark.

I was speechless. My heart was racing but I presented my Penelope with a small smile in saying that it all made sense. For as long as I could remember there was something wrong with my mom. She would be okay one day but then completely off her rocker the next.

Simultaneously, Penelope and I both opened the corresponding birth certificates. Uncle Mark was correct, and it was my assumption that once he found out Bethany's secret, she killed him for it. Penelope stood and rounded on the kitchen – grabbing two tumblers of Crown Royal while I sat the bracelet lovingly on a cloth, rested on the table. There was a lump in my throat and for a slight moment I felt as if I would cry, but I held back the emotion. For the last year and a half of my life, my emotions held me at gunpoint. It was time to relax. This box and its contents are now nothing more than history. Though, I must say that the knowledge that I really never knew my own mother was a shard of glass through my heart. That pain, however residual, will always remain just below the surface – like the smell of a freshly cut lawn. I love the smell of grass.

Time to relax

The weeks flew by and summer became autumn. The leaves turned and lit our afternoons on fire. Slowly, the nights turned cold and I dreamed of a faraway; a faraway that was never cold. I don't just mean cold, like a regular cold. I'm talking about a cold that freezes you to the marrow and refuses to loosen. I loathed the soft hush of winter, with its muffled musings of Norman Rockwell and counterfeit Americana. Give me a beach any day of the year.

Penelope and I took our first step into a new world as she decided to take me up on my offer to move in with me. The living room was full of clothes but I was delighted to see so few boxes and no odd looking modern furniture. As we unpacked, I thought back to that evening at Randolph's. Yes, it was only a hallucination but could I actually be so cruel? I quickly put it out of my mind and moved on.

"Please tell me you're not a cat person." It was a sarcastic question but laced with complete honesty. Being the dog person that

I was, I was thrilled at the notion that Dixie would be moving in too. And though bulldogs are not known for their watchfulness, I was certainly glad for hers that evening when I was jolted awake by her barking obnoxiously at the front door. I bolted up and ran to the front room. Dixie was full of nervous energy as she darted between the bay window and the front door – her paws slapping on the tile. I attempted to calm her but found that her little ticker was working harder than it should be. I asked her, in my usual dog voice, what seemed to be the matter but she just stared up at the front door – panting heavily as if there were someone on the other side.

I gave her a pat on the head and opened the door to show her that there was nothing or no one out there, and at first glance I was correct, but as I turned around to close the door, a reflection of light off the snow caught my eye and I turned back to the door and looked closer. Fear rose as bile bitter in my throat as I stood there and watched. There was someone standing on my front lawn, and... trust me I know how this sounds. They were invisible. No, invisible is not the word. Translucent is more like it. And the more I stared, the more I stood there looking, the less translucent the thing turned out to be. What I mean to say is that the invisible thing was becoming more and more visible with each passing second until it started to take shape. The shape, as it turned out, was human, and not just one human but four: my mother, father, Jillian, and Uncle Mark. It was so strange. They stood there as if they knew I was watching them. The scene played out for nearly an hour and I just watched them. Then, without fanfare, they waved at me then turned and walked away, and it became clear to me what had happened. The finding and opening of the box was the catalyst for their freedom. I waved and went back to bed, certain that I was sleepwalking.

Penelope

Penelope worked her way through a box of glassware and dishes. She had unpacked alone most of the afternoon while Walter was at work. She told him that she would have the rest of it done before he got home. Walter was sure that it would not be and he didn't expect it to be but that's how Penelope was. She was honest and loyal, and sometimes mischievous, especially in bed. Unfortunately for Walter, Penelope could also be deceitful and cunning. With a smile, she placed a full glass bourbon upon the counter and strolled down the hall to the bedroom. There in front of her vanity mirror, she gazed at herself. She picked up a hair brush and began rifling through her hair. And as she did so, her skin became loose and marked with age. Her hair turned silver and brittle. Her hands were gnarled and dry. She smiled again as she heard Walter come in the front door. She slipped the cheap pewter bracelet on her wrist and walked out to greet him.

"Coming, my dear."

"I'm here, darling!"

Afterword

The idea for this story came from a dream I had during an extremely hot summer evening. I awoke with sweat dripping off my face. My hair was drenched and I wondered if all that was around me was real. I strolled into the kitchen for a tall glass of water and then back to bed, where I quickly fell back asleep. The nightmare returned; more intense. It felt as if I were lost in an unknown world; created by a madman aimed at my ultimate demise. When morning came and introduced me to reality, I wrote down all that I could remember. The inspiration of Walter and his family was inspired not by my own family, which would be the norm, but by a mixture of people that I have known throughout my life. The world surrounding Walter may have been fabricated, but the feeling was so real that I shudder to think what another dream might possibly create.

Acknowledgments

This project would not have been possible without the patience and insight of my publisher and editor, Bob Scott. His suggestions and assistance continue to be invaluable. To my children who continue to be an inspiration. And lastly, to all of those who told me that this wasn't possible. Thank you for making me believe in myself.

Also available from Bob Scott Publishing

Serial Blogger by Bob Scott

The killer carefully closed the door to his apartment, inwardly seething after another frustrating day. In the sanctuary of his mind he had spent the day screaming, but to all outwards appearances he had been cool, calm and collected, slightly aloof but quietly and efficiently performing his duties at work. Now, safe in his haven, some of the anger could be released a little.

Some, but not much. Outside was the veneer of civilization, coating both himself and the world at large. Inside was his true thoughts, and the Beast, raging with red claws and bloody fangs against the bars of the cage known to the Beast as Culture, Refinement and Law. Civilization disliked people raging the way the pair wanted to, but something had to give.

Trying to keep within civilized bounds, trying to 'maintain appearances' as his mother would have said, the killer kept his rage non-vocal and as quiet as possible. His cries of rage were silent, and his fists pounding into the furniture were almost so.

But today this would not be enough to satisfy the Beast prowling within him. The killer had suspected as much for some time now, and he struggled to keep it in check. Within his mind he shouted, "Soon, tonight, it will happen!"

The Beast subsided, growling and chafing at the delay. The killer quickly changed into his running clothes and grabbed a backpack he had prepared in advance. Closing the main door to the apartment building, he looked up and down the street, yet not really caring if he was seen. To the casual onlooker he would just be going for one of his usual five mile runs, and in a way that was true. But he was also going hunting, because there was a Beast with a large appetite to feed.

www.ingramcontent.com/pod-product-compliance
Lightning Source LLC
Chambersburg PA
CBHW072226190626
46809CB00017B/980
9781952819124